HEART

OF

ASH

Also by Kim Liggett

Blood and Salt

The Last Harvest

HEART

OF

ASH

KIM LIGGETT

G. P. Putnam's Sons

G. P. PUTNAM'S SONS
an imprint of Penguin Random House LLC
375 Hudson Street
New York, NY 10014

Copyright © 2018 by Kim Liggett.

G. P. Putnam's Sons is a registered trademark of Penguin Random House LLC.
Library of Congress Cataloging-in-Publication Data
Names: Liggett, Kim, author.
Title: Heart of Ash / Kim Liggett.
Description: New York, NY : G. P. Putnam's Sons, [2018] | Sequel to: Blood and salt.
Summary: After escaping the cult that killed her mother in Kansas, Ash starts to search for her missing twin brother, Rhys, and she turns to her immortal mate Dane, who is possessed by the diabolical Coronado, for help.
Identifiers: LCCN 2017013761 (print) | LCCN 2017043760 (ebook) |
ISBN 9780698174016 (ebook) | ISBN 9780399166495 (hardcover)
Subjects: | CYAC: Supernatural—Fiction. | Immortality—Fiction. | Love—Fiction. |
Twins—Fiction. | Brothers and sisters—Fiction.
Classification: LCC PZ7.1.L54 (ebook) | LCC PZ7.1.L54 He 2018 (print) |
DDC [Fic]—dc23
LC record available at https://lccn.loc.gov/2017013761

Printed in the United States of America.
ISBN 9780399166495
1 3 5 7 9 10 8 6 4 2

Design by Jaclyn Reyes. Text set in Bell MT.

For Maddie and Rahm

It ended with forever

1

STANDING OVER THE dried-up bed of Quivira grass, I pricked the tip of my finger. Blood rushed to the surface as if aching for escape.

Dripping onto the neglected soil, I watched the dark green color creep up every blade, making it lush again. Making it new.

How I longed to be a blade of that grass.

But I would never change. Never die. Because I was immortal.

Lying down, feeling the crush of the blades against my back, I couldn't help but think of my mother. This twelve-by-twelve-foot raised bed of sod in my mother's studio was always her favorite part of the house. She grew it herself from seeds that came from Quivira, Kansas, the cult where she grew up. It was lush and strong now, but it would be dried up, dead as a doornail, by tomorrow evening. All it took was one drop of my blood to make it come to life, to pretend I was still there, at the edge of the corn, listening to the stalks hulk and sway like a churning sea.

If I closed my eyes, I swore I could still feel my five-hundred-year-old ancestor cutting into me, claiming me as a vessel for her soul, her memories unfolding in my bloodstream like a poem of heartbreak, betrayal, and revenge.

Normally, I wouldn't let myself delve into this kind of madness, but this was a day for remembering.

One year ago today, my brother, Rhys, and I tracked our mother to Quivira, thinking we were going to save her from giving her body over to Katia in some ancient ritual, when *I* was the one Katia wanted all along.

And like a fool, I met a boy there—a beautiful, treacherous boy—who I not only gave my heart to, but chose to blood bind to, making him my immortal mate. The same boy who lied to me, killed my ancestors by leading them into a possessed, bloodthirsty field of corn, and also happened to be marked as a vessel for Coronado's soul, Katia's former lover and enemy.

While my mother sacrificed herself for me, using her light, her love, to rip Katia's soul from my body, Dane didn't have anyone to save him from that fate. I watched Coronado take over his body—infect his mind. And I knew only too well what it was like having another person's soul inside of you—an unrelenting darkness.

And because without darkness there can be no light, my twin brother got the flip side of the coin. While my blood has the power to heal, Rhys's blood carries pure death, which we found out the hard way when he accidently got a drop of blood on our friend Beth and nearly killed her. I was able to heal her with my own blood, but the look of horror on his face when he realized what he was capable of haunted me. He took off running into the corn and that was the last time I saw him.

A dark ripple of energy rushed through me at the thought. I tried to shake it, but it never really left me.

It made me wonder whether something got left behind—a rotting organ? A memento mori? I half expected to cut myself open and find Katia living inside of me, but I'd witnessed her soul enter my mother's body. I'd watched them turn to ash as I slipped the dagger into her heart. The darkness I felt had to be my own. Sometimes it seemed as if my mother's light was the only thing keeping the darkness at bay . . . keeping me from becoming just like Katia. A monster.

All I knew was that everything I ever loved or hated had been taken from me in one fell swoop.

"Morning, sunshine!" Beth chirped as she flung open the drapes, flooding my mother's studio with light.

Well, almost everything.

Gripping the grass, I pulled myself to a sitting position.

Strange, I felt a deeper connection to that tiny plot of grass than anything else on this waking earth. As much as I hated Quivira and everything it stood for, I'd left a part of my soul there—the good part—my innocence. And I wasn't quite ready to let that go.

I held up my hand in front of me, the sun glinting off the tiny particles of gold dust that clung to my skin. I used to think the gold was beautiful on my mother. Now it just reminded me of the sacrifice she'd made—her parting gift that was carved into my skin. The alchemical formula for making gold.

My body was covered in scars no one could see. Some that would never heal.

I ran my hands over my arms, my chest, settling on the scar below my collarbone—the last tattoo my mother gave me—a circle with a dot in the center, the alchemy symbol for gold or sun. I didn't dare let my fingertips drift any lower, to the place where I'd cut myself so I could become blood bound to Dane.

"Isn't it lovely?" Beth said as she stared across the muddy Hudson.

"Sure." I inspected my newly healed finger. "Another great day to be alive."

"I'll say!" She grinned back at me.

I wish there were a dimmer switch for Beth. It seemed like the more miserable I was, the more manic her happiness became, but she was probably always the same, which meant I was getting worse.

"You know what today is?" Beth asked as she began to straighten up the mess of perfume vials and testing strips scattered around the studio. She knew better than to ask what I was working on. It was embarrassing for both of us, like discovering a drug addict in the midst of their addiction. It was my dirty little secret, how I kept trying to capture Dane's scent, but I could never get it exactly right. It tortured me.

"Yes. Of course, I know what today is," I whispered. "It's the one-year anniversary of when my mother disappeared . . . the beginning of the end."

4

"Oh my stars! Is that right? Well, it's also Saturday. The day you said I could finally ride the subway."

"Look." I exhaled a measured breath. "We have a driver. He'll take you anywhere you want to go."

"I don't know where I want to go. That's the whole point. I want to let the rails decide."

"You're not a hobo in a forties movie," I said.

"Oh, wouldn't that be grand!"

"Yeah. Super." I brushed the lush blades of grass from my palms. "But I can't risk something happening to you."

"I know all the rules," she said as she bounced on the balls of her feet. "We've been over them a million times. This is my no-no square—you can't touch me there. Stranger danger. Don't look people in the eyes. Just say no. Nine-one-one. I've got a rape whistle and pepper spray. I can do this. I know the subway map like the bottom of my foot."

I couldn't help but smile at that. I don't think she messed up the words. I *literally* think Beth knows all the lines on the bottom of her foot.

"Pretty please," she trilled as she skipped around the raised bed of grass like a deranged six-year-old.

"Fine," I groaned. Anything to get her to stop.

"Thank you, thank you, Ash!" She hurled herself on top of me.

I got out from under her and made my way over to the work-table, squinting up at the bottles lining the shelves.

It was thrilling at first, figuring out the formula and making the gold. But with each ingot poured, it reminded me that time

5

was passing. I wonder if that's how my mother felt at the end. Spent and worried, as she waited for Katia to come for her.

But it didn't look like anyone was coming for me. Including Dane or Coronado or whatever he was.

Not even my own brother. My twin.

When Beth and I left Quivira and drove to New York City, I kept thinking it was only a matter of time before Rhys returned. My brother was a creature of habit. But days turned into weeks. Weeks turned into months. I'd made enough gold to last ten lifetimes by now, hired the best private investigators, but Rhys never surfaced. My brother could hold a grudge like nobody's business, but this was different. He either hated me so much he couldn't bear to see me again or he felt like a monster. A killer, which is something Rhys wouldn't be able to bear. He couldn't even kill a roach. We'd have to capture it and take it to a park to release it.

I kept thinking maybe he had amnesia—that one day he'd fall out of bed and suddenly remember who he was and come home, like some cheesy Lifetime movie, but deep down I knew it wasn't that simple.

"Come downstairs." Beth smoothed her hand over my shoulder. "Let me make you something to eat."

"No, I'm fine." I pulled out a pound of lead from the scrap pile. "I want to make another dozen ingots today."

"Okeydokey," she said as she turned to go downstairs. "An omelet it is."

I opened my mouth to argue, but there was no point. Beth

only heard what she wanted to hear, or it was sent through a filter process I just didn't understand—like some rickety game of Mouse Trap with a few of the pieces missing.

I was all set to ignore her when I sensed a dark shadow pass over me. Looking up at the padlocked skylight, I shivered in the warmth. I knew it was probably just a pigeon, but it spooked me. I recalled last year when I came home to find my mother gone and the studio full of crows. Coronado's crows. The ones who followed him wherever he went, like an omen of doom.

"Be right down," I called to Beth, my voice betraying me with a slight waver.

My walk quickly turned into a run.

Slamming the steel door shut behind me, I took in shallow gulps of air.

Slipping my hand into my pocket, I felt the black silk ribbon graze my fingertips. This was the same black silk ribbon Katia gave to me, that came alive when I met Dane. But maybe the ribbon was reacting to Katia's blood inside of me, reaching out for Coronado's blood inside of Dane. And now that Katia was gone, so was its magic.

I coiled my finger around the black strand and a flash of remembrance came over me—Dane under Heartbreak Tree, the place of our blood binding. His hands in my hair. Limbs entwined. The ribbon dancing all around us. And for a moment, I thought I felt something, but it was only a trick of the senses, a phantom limb. The black strand was lifeless in my hand, a cold, dead memory of another time, another place, another life.

7

Untangling my fingers from the ribbon, I buried it as deep in my pocket as it would go. I should've left it behind long ago, but it wasn't just a symbol of my tumultuous love affair . . . it was a reminder of my undoing, how easily I was led into Dane's arms. And that's something I couldn't allow myself to forget. Because of my foolishness, I'd torn my family to shreds. I didn't deserve to forget.

I told myself the bird passing overhead was probably just déjà vu, but I couldn't afford to ignore my instincts. Not anymore.

I ignored them once before, and look where that got me.

2

DESCENDING THE WROUGHT-IRON spiral stairs to the kitchen, I found Beth flitting around, singing that stupid Backstreet Boys song. "'Tell me why-eee / ain't nothing but a heartache / tell me why-eee.'"

I shot her a murderous glare; she clamped her hand over her mouth.

"I'm so sorry," she said through her fingers. "It's really catchy."

"Uncatch it, please." I sat down at the kitchen table, trying to forget that was Dane's secret favorite song. That alone should've been enough of a warning signal, but no. Thumbing through the paper, I noticed the best section was missing. Beth probably found a coupon for skydiving or pickles. God only knows.

Beth and I had fallen into this mundane routine: Sometimes it felt like I was the grumpy husband and Beth was the 1950s housewife, full of sunshine and diet pills.

"What's up with the paper?"

When she didn't reply, I looked over to find her frozen, mid–egg crack, staring at the wall. She got stuck like this sometimes. Every once in a while Beth would get a vision. At first, I desperately wanted to know what she saw, what she felt, thinking her visions would be the key to finding Rhys. Like that time she dreamed of a chipped tooth on the water fountain at the Central Park Zoo. Rhys and I used to go there all the time. That fountain was our meet-up spot if we were ever separated. Beth and I waited out there for days, looking for a sign or a trace of my brother, but when she accidentally chipped her own tooth on the fountain, I realized it was *her* future she was seeing. Nothing more than a place she wanted to go—a tourist attraction from a guidebook she'd picked up at a Jersey rest stop. She didn't even want to get her tooth fixed. Her seer skills were slowly coming back, but everything was still pretty scrambled.

"I bet Rhys will like my omelets, too." Beth startled me as she set down the scorched eggs in front of me. "I mean . . . we already know he likes my muffins."

I forced myself to take a huge bite. "Yeah . . . yum."

It pained me the way she talked about Rhys, like he'd just gone out for orange juice. We never spoke of it, but I knew Beth slept in my brother's room. I guess we both needed our little secrets.

As soon as she turned her back, I spit it out in my napkin.

Ever since I gave her my blood in Quivira, to save her from the effects of Rhys's blood, I swore she could sense my mood. It's nothing like the connection Dane and I shared, but it was there; I was a part of her. If she felt even a fraction of my misery, she certainly did a good job of hiding it.

But Rhys and I shared blood, as well. I wondered why I couldn't feel him in the same way. I knew he was out there . . . I knew he was alive, but when I thought of him, when I reached out to him, I just felt numb. It was as if he'd disappeared off the face of the earth. Maybe he was so horrified by what his blood could do that he was hiding out in a cave somewhere, but that was probably unlikely. His only survival skill was knowing how to operate a two-thousand-dollar espresso machine. But who knows, maybe I'd underestimated him; I always had. And he'd always overestimated me.

The air-conditioning came on, making the chandelier quiver. "Ash?"

I tore my eyes away from the shimmering glass. "What?"

"Maybe I should stay here with you today," Beth said, her brow knotted up. "We can watch movies . . . or I can help you work."

The idea of Beth hanging around all day trying to cheer me up was too torturous to contemplate.

"No." I tossed my napkin onto my plate, trying to hide the rest of my mutilated omelet. "I said you can ride the subway and that's what you should do. But you better hurry if you want to hit the brunch crowd. That's when all the fun happens."

"Really? Well, if you're sure it's okay." She squeezed my shoulder before skipping back to my room to get changed.

As soon as she disappeared, I jumped up to toss the rest of the food and spotted the missing section of the newspaper wadded up in the trash can.

"That's odd," I whispered.

Beth was a recycling tyrant. I dug it up, smoothing it out on the cold marble countertop. Page Six—a rare two-page spread on Dane Coronado, heir to the Arcanum Corporation. BILLIONAIRE PLAYBOY TO ATTEND THE NEW YORK PUBLIC LIBRARY PATRONS BALL. WHO WILL BE HIS LUCKY DATE—OR DATES? Beneath was a photo of Dane surrounded by gorgeous models at the Cannes Film Festival. A blistering heat rose from the pit of my stomach, shooting through every cell in my body.

Beth skipped back into the room.

Crumpling up the paper, I jabbed it down into goopy eggshells and yogurt so I wouldn't be tempted to dig it out again. Nothing good could come of me thinking about Dane or Coronado or whatever the hell he was.

"I'm ready." Beth twirled around in a sundress dotted with tiny daisies.

"No way." I shook my head. "You're not wearing that."

"I thought I looked nice."

"You do, but that's not something you wear when you're alone . . . on the subway. Trust me. You don't want that kind of attention." I grabbed her hand, leading her into Rhys's room. Snatching an ugly plaid button-down shirt from his closet, I tossed it to her. "Put this on."

"You want me to wear Rhys's shirt?"

"I'm sorry, I didn't even think—"

"No, it's not that. I love being near Rhys and his things, but it's pretty warm outside."

"Exactly. You don't want to get sunburned."

Beth grinned and wagged her finger at me. "You're such a smarty." As I led her to the elevator, she said, "Oh, and don't forget about your meeting with Mr. Timmons."

I bristled at the thought. Alexander Timmons, Esq. All those years I thought he was just my mom's lawyer—turns out, not only was he brokering the gold ingots for her, generating fake papers, and laundering our money, he was also my mother's secret boyfriend and madly in love with her.

Looking back, it seemed odd that he was around for all our birthdays, holidays. We just thought my mother was his favorite client. And then some. After I came back from Quivira, I started going through her things and found a box of love letters. Things I will never be able to unsee. I couldn't believe she hid that from us. But then again—she was also hiding the fact that we had blood ties to an immortal.

"Just try to be nice to him this time," Beth said as she got in the elevator. "He's trying to help."

"With what we're paying him, I don't really have to be nice."

"Ash." She gave me a look.

"Fine. I'll try. But it's still . . . *weird.*"

"Weird is good, right?" she said as she waved.

I pasted on a smile for Beth's benefit and stood there waving back like an idiot until the doors finally came to a close.

Letting out a burst of pent-up air, I allowed my shoulders to fall into their familiar slouch.

I decided to tidy up a bit, but who was I kidding? It was only an excuse to open the garbage can again. In one year, Coronado had managed to stage his own death and present Dane as his long-lost nephew, his heir, so he could take his place in the Arcanum Corporation and start anew.

Dane had caused quite a sensation in the media. When you're that good-looking, single, *and* a billionaire, I guess it kind of goes with the territory. Coronado was probably just showing off his new body. It'd been a long time since he'd been able to operate out in the open, but he was certainly playing it up. Magazine covers, photo ops. I knew it was Coronado running the show, pulling the strings, but there were times when I swore I could still feel Dane. When Katia was inside of me, even for that brief moment, all I felt was darkness. Peering down at the only bit of exposed newspaper, I focused on Dane's hand.

When I closed my eyes, I could feel his touch. I could feel his thumb dragging across my hip bone. An unexpected warmth rushed over my skin.

I took my foot off the lever, making the can snap shut.

"Don't be pathetic, Ash."

3

BY THE TIME Timmons arrived, I'd been stewing for hours.

I almost felt bad for the shit storm he was about to walk into.

Almost.

Timmons stepped out of the elevator, reeking of Ivy League—khakis, loafers, starched dress shirt, preppy tie with a blue blazer. He looked like he should be headed for a polo match, not brokering gold for the underworld. God only knows what landed him in this kind of work, but he was connected. Fake papers for Beth in under twenty-four hours, restraining orders in place, ready to file against Dane Coronado if he started harassing me, but it never came to that. It never came to anything.

It made me wonder if Quivira ever even happened. If Dane ever happened.

Seeing his photo like that this morning took me by surprise; it was like getting sucker punched, but it went deeper than that.

I could cut myself off from the world, but in a single breath, a fraction of a second, I'd think of his hands, his gaze on my skin, and a traitorous warmth would bloom in my chest, as if I were seeing him for the first time. And now he was coming to New York City. In the past year, he'd made no attempt to contact me. Fired no warning shot. All of Coronado's talk about forever, how he'd always know where to find me. Was that just some bullshit line? Wouldn't put it past either one of them. Because here he was in *my* hometown, like it was nothing. Like *I* was nothing.

Timmons let out a measured sigh as he stared down at the stack of fresh ingots.

I didn't know what my mother told him about all that, but he probably thought she was some sexy international thief and I'd taken over the trade. Not an immortal freak making tons of gold so I could have the resources to find my twin, who carried pure death in his blood. That part he didn't know.

"We're going to have to slow down a bit," Timmons said as he set his attaché on the table. "There's only so much known gold in the world, Ash. We've moved on to private collectors. It's getting harder and harder to turn this into clean money."

"So turn it into dirty money," I said as I poured myself a cup of tea.

"That's not how Nina—"

"My mother's dead," I snapped. "I'm in charge now. If you don't like it, you can find another job."

"This isn't just a job to me."

"Believe me, I know all about it."

The slightest hint of a blush crept up over the collar of his shirt. "We should've told you. I'm sorry you had to find out that way, but I loved her. I promised Nina that I would always look out for you. No matter what."

"Great," I said as I looked away, trying not to get choked up. "Then you'll do this for me."

"You have plenty of money; why not slow down, stay safe?"

"I don't know what kind of shape Rhys will be in when I find him," I said, thinking about what his blood could do.

"Does this have something to do with Dane Coronado?"

"You tell me." I met his eyes, trying to stare the truth out of him.

"I have information for you." He took a seat, digging a folder out of his attaché.

"Finally," I said as I took a sip of my tea. I wondered how long it was going to take him to tell me my enemy was in town. I snatched the folder off the table, bracing myself for Dane's face to be staring back at me, but what I found shook me to my core.

A man splayed out on a Persian rug, blood seeping from his nose, his mouth . . . his pores. Just like Betsy, Tommy, and Henry at Quivira—the victims of my brother's blood.

"You asked me to keep an eye on deaths of this nature, people bleeding out from unknown causes, but without wounds."

"Where was this?" I managed to ask. "When did this happen?"

"Six days ago in Lisbon."

"Is that Ambassador Wells?" I studied the photo. "I think I read about him in the paper, but they said he died of natural causes."

"Since when do you believe everything you read?"

I shot him a look. "This has to be related to the Perry death from last month, and the Rhinebeck case before that."

"Three prominent men. Old, wealthy families. Same manner of death. I'd say it's a pretty big coincidence, wouldn't you?"

My breath hitched in my throat. "Any sign of Rhys?"

He rubbed the back of his neck. "For the life of me, I can't understand why you'd think Rhys would be connected to something like this. I've known Rhys since he was a child. He couldn't hurt a fly."

"Just answer the question."

He swallowed hard as he rummaged through his papers. "No one even *slightly* resembling Rhys was seen entering or leaving the residences of any one of these people." He leaned forward. "Don't you think it's time you fill me in on whatever's *really* going on?"

Studying him carefully, I said, "That's funny, I was about to ask you the same thing. Why don't you open the trash can?"

"Okay." He looked slightly amused at first, but as he stepped over to the stainless steel cylinder, I watched a bead of sweat trail down his temple.

Clearly, Timmons has had some scarier clients than me.

Standing as far away as possible, he pressed his foot on the pedal. Peeking inside, I watched the blood leach from his face. "Before you jump to conclusions, let me exp—"

"You knew," I said as I refilled my cup, just to keep myself occupied so I wouldn't wring his neck. "Why didn't you tell me?"

"I didn't want to upset you," he said as he rolled up the sleeve of his dress shirt, cringing as he reached in through the layers of goop to retrieve it.

"I told you this man is a threat."

"With all due respect," he said as he carefully laid the soggy paper on the counter, "I've been watching his every move for the past year. Whatever happened between the two of you seems to be in the past," Timmons said, eyeing the leggy models flanking Dane's side in the photo.

I broke the cup in my hand, and blood began dripping to the floor.

He rushed toward me.

I tried to hide the wound, but my skin healed so fast it expelled the fine bone china from the fleshy part of my palm.

I expected Timmons to freak, but his face lit up as if he'd just discovered the last piece of an elaborate puzzle. He wiped the blood from my hand with his handkerchief. "So, it's true. All of it. *You* were the vessel. Not your mother."

"How do you know about that?" I exhaled shakily.

"Nina told me everything. But I had no idea. Is that why you've changed so much? Are you Katia?"

"No." I yanked my hand away from him. "I'm nothing like Katia. My mother sacrificed herself to save me from Katia. Does that make you feel differently about me?" I said as I gathered the stray bits of china off the floor and dumped them in the trash. "It should."

"No. Of course not," he said. "That sounds like something she would do. She loved you and Rhys more than anything."

The mere mention of the two of them in the same sentence brought an ache to my chest, like pressing down on broken ribs.

Timmons picked up a gold ingot, inspecting my signature mark. "You know, you can always sell your blood if you need another revenue stream."

"What?"

"There are rumors. Along with medical research and pharmaceuticals, the Arcanum owns a very exclusive wellness-care line—supplements, serums, that kind of thing. Extremely expensive. But it's done."

"Wait . . . so Coronado's been selling his blood?"

"Not just Coronado," he said as he set down the gold bar. "The Arcanum is a collective. Dane Coronado is only the face of the company. Apparently, there's a group of immortals who run things; they call themselves *the council.*"

"Hold up . . ." I braced myself against the table. "There are other immortals?" I knew there was at least one spiritual immortal out there, but I had no idea there was an entire consortium. If Katia achieved her immortality through alchemy; I guess it makes sense that there would be others. "Who are they?"

"That's the billion-dollar question. I can put out some feelers, see if I can get any more information, names."

"Please," I whispered as I stared down at Dane's face.

"I knew that Coronado was immortal," Timmons said as he caught my gaze. "But is this boy—"

"Coronado's vessel," I replied. "His blood relative. But Dane wasn't so lucky. He didn't have anyone to save him."

"And you loved him," he said, his eyes misting over.

"It's a little more complicated than that."

"I was in love with your mother. I understand complicated. Try me."

In that moment, I decided to tell Timmons everything, not because I thought he could help me; I just wanted him to understand how truly fucked I was.

"Well, let's see . . . Dane lied to me, broke my heart, oh, and he led my entire bloodline—Larkin men, women, and children—into a field of bloodthirsty corn, to their deaths. And that was all *before* Coronado took over his body."

"Bastard," he managed to whisper.

"But he saved me, too. If it wasn't for Dane, Coronado would've killed me on our first night in Quivira. And now, because of me, Dane's a vessel—a living, breathing skin suit for Francisco Vásquez de Coronado's soul."

"I see," he said with a knitted brow. "But I still don't understand how this has anything to do with Rhys."

"You know how my mom used to say without darkness there can be no light?"

"Of course."

"Rhys and I are twins. The light and the dark. While my blood has the power to heal, Rhys's has the power to kill. The people who had contact with even a drop of Rhys's blood died exactly like that," I said, my eyes drifting to the crime-scene photo.

21

"Okay." He let out a gust of pent-up air as he sank down in the chair, loosening his tie, looking like he was about to pass out.

"I knew I shouldn't have said anything," I said as I went to get him a bottle of water.

"No . . . no, it's not that," he said as he took a deep swig. "It's just . . . I didn't know if this was relevant before, but now I'm not so sure."

"What? What is it?"

With trembling hands, he removed a slip of paper from one of his folders.

"We're not the only ones interested in these deaths. Another party has linked them together as well; they even requested the same surveillance footage. It took some doing, but I tracked the IP address to the Arcanum Corporation, which your friend Mr. Dane Coronado is a part of," he said as he handed me the paper. "It could be a coincidence."

I traced my finger over the IP address. "Believe me. There are no coincidences when it comes to this man."

"I believe you," he said as he squeezed my hand. "I'll give you some time to think about it, how you want to proceed, but in the meantime, I'll do some digging, see what I can come up with on the council."

He kept his head down as he made his way to the elevator. I'd never seen Timmons speechless before, but I was grateful. I didn't think I could stand listening to him try to tell me everything was going to be all right.

With Timmons gone, I went back to the kitchen, eyeing the

newspaper, the photo of Dane. I remembered the last time I saw him, at the sacred circle in Quivira; it was Dane's body, but Coronado's words. He said it was in both of our interests that Rhys be found. I didn't understand what he meant at the time, but now that I knew the Arcanum were tracking the same mysterious deaths, they must've suspected my brother's involvement as well. But what was Coronado's interest in all of this?

Even though I knew Dane was gone, seeing him, in the flesh, was going to be hard; but if Coronado knew anything about my brother, I had to find out.

Maybe it was time to rattle some cages.

Starting with my own.

4

I SENT BETH an SOS message, asking her to meet me on the corner at six p.m., sharp. I knew she wouldn't ask why. Beth was like a Labrador puppy; she'd go anywhere, anytime.

I started to get ready—like *ready*-ready, with mascara and everything—but stopped myself. "What the hell are you doing? It's not a date." I scrubbed off the makeup and took off the dress. Digging through the pile of clothes on my bed, I opted for a pair of black jeans and an old Pretenders T-shirt with a hoodie. Pulling my tangled mass of hair into a bun, I secured it with the black ribbon and headed for the elevator. I didn't want to give myself even a fraction of a second to change my mind, but when the doors opened, I froze.

I couldn't even remember the last time I'd ventured outside.

That was one of the perks of living in New York City. You could get everything delivered. I didn't even have to see the delivery guys; at my request the doorman sent it up on the elevator so I could pull it off, like some kind of feral animal. Sometimes I felt like a space traveler, living in a pod above a hostile planet, only I'm the one who felt hostile. I didn't know what I was capable of. Sometimes the darkness felt as gentle as a whisper and other times it would flare up without warning, a dark and wild energy pulsing through my fingertips. I didn't know if this is what it felt like to be immortal or if it was something else entirely. Unfortunately, Katia didn't exactly leave me a guidebook for this shit.

Swallowing the boulder-sized lump in my throat, I stepped onto the elevator. I was afraid to look at my reflection in the floor-to-ceiling mirrors, afraid of what I might see. Katia . . . my mother . . . Rhys. I was surrounded by ghosts.

As soon as the elevator doors opened, I propelled myself out of the stifling metal box, making a beeline for the front door. Our doorman backed up against the wall as if he were seeing a phantom, which wasn't completely off base. "N-nice to see you, Miss Larkin. Hope you have a—"

I pulled up my hoodie and hightailed it to Broadway. I'm sure I looked like a strung-out mess, but no one seemed to notice or care. This was New York City, where eye contact was considered a disease.

The city was hot; not Kansas hot, but the sidewalks retained the heat. The summer garbage piling up, people sweating . . . the whole city was ripe. And with my heightened sense of smell, it was a challenge, to say the least.

Beth was waiting for me on the corner, Rhys's flannel shirt tied around her waist, a huge grin plastered across her face.

I braced myself as she lurched forward, giving me one of those ridiculous bear hugs, and I swore I could smell the sunshine on her skin.

"You've been to the High Line," I said.

"How did you know?"

I could smell the Chelsea Market spices, the Hudson River, the old rusted tracks, and even the men who put them there, but I didn't want to creep her out. "Because you went to Doughnuttery." I pointed to her bag.

"Oh, they have the most wonderful sweets."

"They're doughnuts."

"But look," she said as she opened the bag and shoved it under my nose like a two-year-old. "No nuts."

I pulled away from the sickeningly sweet smell. "Do you have to eat those now?"

"Nope." She crammed the bag into her backpack and pulled a half-eaten wad of cotton candy from her pocket, cramming it into her mouth.

"We might want to take you to the dentist."

"Okeydokey," she said as she followed. "What's that?"

"Someone who looks at your teeth."

"Ooh, that sounds like fun. I don't think anyone's looked at my teeth before, except at the breeding ceremony."

"I'm not even touching that one." I shook my head. "The dentist is a blast. You'll love it. So, how was your first solo subway trip?" I asked, trying to keep my mind occupied as we made our way to the park.

26

"So fun." She skipped ahead of me. "I made lots of friends."

"Oh God. Please tell me you didn't give out our home address?"

"Heavens, no. I remember the rules, but they all want to meet you. They're having a get-together tonight . . . under the bridge."

"Under the bridge? Yeah, no more solo trips on the subway for you. I told you people aren't really friendly here—"

"Beth!" A burly guy, his neck covered in tattoos, waved his arms as he crossed the street.

I squared my body, ready for anything.

"How's Biddy?" Beth smiled warmly as she stepped around me.

"I tried the radish greens, just like you said, and she's back to normal."

"That's great."

"Shoot. My bus is here," he said as he looked back. "Gotta run. See you around, angel."

"What was that about?" I glared at him as he got on the M7.

"Biddy, his tortoise. She was awfully sick because he was giving her too much fruit."

"Beth," I lectured as we entered Central Park, "I really don't think you should talk to strangers. This isn't Quivira, or Kansas, for that matter. You should really—"

"Beth." A woman with all of two teeth called out, her wizened claw beckoning us over to her domain—a bench, covered in pigeon shit and God only knows what else.

"Hi, Mrs. Dolenz." Beth dragged me over there.

"How do you know all these people anyway?"

"Just from around the neighborhood."

"Well, it's annoying. It's like going on a walk with the mayor."

"Oh, Mr. De Blasio? He's a peach."

"You know the mayor? Of course you do." I let out a deep sigh.

I thought Beth would be overwhelmed here, but she seemed to thrive on the energy. As many talks as I'd given her on stranger danger, she embraced the city with open arms, and the city did the same for Beth. She belonged here, more than Rhys and I ever did. Maybe Beth belongs everywhere.

"This is my best friend, Ash," Beth said as she pulled me forward.

"Nice to meet you," I said.

Mrs. Dolenz's beady eyes raked over me. "I know you. You used to walk down my path every day . . . with a boy."

"My brother, Rhys," I said, feeling a stab of remorse. "You haven't seen him, have you?"

"Strange." Her eyes narrowed. "You're the second person to ask me that today."

"What?" I took a step closer. "Who else asked about my brother?"

"I couldn't say."

I got right up in her face.

"Ash," Beth hissed at me. "She's blind."

"Oh." I took a step back. "Well, what was his voice like?"

"Crushed velvet." A winsome smile took over her face. "There was an accent, but I couldn't say from where. But aren't you going to ask me what he smelled like?"

"How'd you—"

"I may be blind, but I have the senses of a pit viper. He smelled like the woods and oranges."

I looked around the park, searching for him, when I caught a different, eerily familiar scent. Mold and dander, city grit beneath calcified nails. And once I knew what to look for, they were everywhere.

In the sky, scattered across the lawn, under benches, in the trees, their piercing eyes glaring down at us from on high.

"Crow." The word escaped my lips. The whisperer of secrets. The harbinger of death. "Coronado."

5

"ASH, SLOW DOWN," Beth called after me. "Talk to me. I wanted to tell you . . . I did, but—"

"There's no time for that," I said as I plunged headfirst into the crowd in front of the New York Public Library. This was beyond hurt feelings. Beyond my pride. "He might know something about Rhys."

"What are you going to do?" Beth asked as she struggled to keep up.

When I realized I had no plan, I stopped short, sending Beth crashing into me. Getting out the door and going to the library was as far as my brilliant strategizing had gotten me. The old Ash would've been on the ball—she would've scored tickets to the event, made an entrance—but no, here I was in jeans and a T-shirt, surrounded by paparazzi, people taking selfies, couples kissing. The whole scene made me want to gag.

"I'll know what to do when I see him," I said as I elbowed our way to the front of the barricade.

"Please don't be reckless," Beth said nervously as the limos began to arrive. "You don't have anything sharp, do you?

"Why didn't I think of that?" I teased. "All I have is this ribbon," I said as I pulled it from my hair and secured it around my wrist. "I guess I can always use it to strangle him."

The guy standing next to me—husky, middle-aged, with a Hello Kitty autograph book—looked at me with wide eyes.

"JK." I flashed a saccharine smile.

He let out a nervous chuckle before returning to his sweating and catcalling.

"Ash, I'm serious." Beth clung to my arm. "If you lose your temper, you could end up exposing him, exposing yourself as immortal. I know what he did was wrong, but Dane is my friend."

I looked at her sharply. "Dane is gone."

"You don't really believe that or you wouldn't be here. Dane saved my life—took care of me when no one else would. And he *loved* you."

I stared straight ahead into the blur of flashing lights. It hurt to hear her speak of him that way . . . to speak of him at all. It hadn't occurred to me how torn she must've felt. Beth was loyal to a fault. Loyal to Quivira. Loyal to Rhys. Loyal to me. And like it or not, loyal to Dane.

Maybe Beth was right to be nervous. I had no idea what seeing him would do to me. It was the ultimate test. Could I be in his presence without wanting to kiss him or tear his throat open?

A sleek black Jaguar pulled up. Cameras were flashing; girls were screaming. A dashing figure emerged and I knew it was him. The way he stood, the way he walked, the way he lowered his chin as if he were on the verge of blushing from all the attention. I thought he'd look odd in a tux, out of place, but he wore it with the same casual confidence as the homespun clothes he was wearing when we first met at the junkyard. Frantically, I searched for signs of Coronado's presence, but all I saw was Dane. All I felt was Dane. The Dane I remembered; the Dane who broke my heart. Could it be possible that he was somehow able to gain control? "Is that really you?" I whispered.

As he turned to ascend the stairs, two gorgeous women trailed after him. I didn't know if one was his date, or both, or if they were just handlers. But I didn't like it. I couldn't believe he was going to slip in and out of town like I was some girl he met at a bar once. I wanted to scream out, *We're blood bound, you asshole*, but thought better of it.

With each step he took away from me, my heart receded deeper into my chest, as if it were crawling back into darkness.

But then Dane stopped, glancing over his shoulder.

I felt his gaze slip over my skin like warm, liquid fingers.

Ducking behind a group of photographers, I took in a shuddering breath.

Even in this strange place, a sea of concrete and flashing

lights between us, my blood seemed to shimmer in my veins, as if it were reaching out for him.

Whether it was Dane or Coronado, I knew it would be hard seeing him in the flesh.

I knew it would open old wounds.

But I didn't expect to want him all over again.

And that wrecked me more than anything.

6

JUST AS I was catching my breath, praying I wasn't spotted, Beth started waving frantically. "Over here, Dane! It's Ash and Beth!"

I grabbed her arm, pulling it down, but when I looked back toward the steps, he was gone.

If Dane saw us, he certainly wasn't going out of his way to acknowledge it. What did I expect? That he'd wade through the crowd and take me in his arms? The fact that that was the first thing that popped in my head made me cringe.

"What is it?" Beth asked.

"Nothing." I shook it off. "Look, we have to figure out how to get inside and—"

"Come with us," a man said as he gripped my elbow. There was another one standing next to Beth.

"Great. That Hello Kitty asshole must've ratted me out," I

muttered to Beth. "Officers, look, I'm not a threat to anyone. It was an innocent comment."

"And even if she did strangle her boyfriend, he wouldn't die. It's a long story, but—"

"He's not my boyfriend," I interrupted. "Not anymore."

The guard hanging on to me looked me up and down. "Confirmed," he said as he touched his Bluetooth.

"They don't believe me! Of course they don't. Oh my God, you think I'm crazy, don't you?" I laughed. "Okay, look," I said as I dug my phone out of my pocket. "I'm just going to call my lawyer. He'll straighten—"

The security guy snatched the phone out of my hand and slipped it into his pocket.

"Hey—"

"Oh, she's telling the truth," Beth chimed in. "Timmons, that's her lawyer, but it turns out he was also her mom's lover, but her mom had to sacrifice herself to this really mean lady who was trying to take over Ash's body."

"Beth." I glowered at her.

"Oh, sorry. Did I do the TMT again?"

"TMT?"

"Too much talk."

As they pulled us around the side of the building, where catering trucks and limos were jamming up Forty-First Street, I was trying to figure out a means of escape, but when I saw they were taking us past the security barricade, inside the library for questioning, I stopped resisting. They were taking us exactly where we needed to be. Once I got inside, maybe I could cause a disturbance, flush him out. I knew this library inside and out from when Rhys and I used to play hide-and-seek in the stacks as kids. One time, Rhys hid inside the utility closet near the Rose Room. The one you can't open from the inside. He was only trapped in there for three minutes, but I don't think he ever got over it.

The two security guards led us up a back stairwell, up three flights, to an elaborately carved wood door. Just as I was getting ready to bite his hand and tell Beth to run, they let go of us and opened the doors.

As Beth pulled me forward, I caught the raised edge of the mark on the guard's wrist, the crow, wings outstretched. "Arcanum," I whispered. By the time I realized what was happening, it was too late. We were standing smack-dab in the center of one of the most prestigious parties in New York City.

I tried to tug on the door, but they were barring the exit. My plan was to surprise him, so I could keep the upper hand, but Dane had been expecting me. He knew I'd take the bait, and like the eternal fool, I'd played right into his hands.

7

I'D BEEN IN the Rose Room during the day a million times to study, but never at night. There was something even more magical about it. The long heavy oak tables had been pushed aside to make room for a full orchestra. There were white gardenias and peonies everywhere. Movie stars and fashionistas, dressed to kill. At least Beth had on a sundress. I didn't even look good enough to be mistaken for one of the staff. People were staring, and not in a good way. Beth urged me to at least pull down my hoodie. As soon as I did, I got a glimpse of my hair in one of the ornate gilded mirrors and almost burst out laughing.

"This isn't how I wanted to do this, not by a long shot, but we might as well get it over with."

"Okeydokey. I'll look for him over here first," Beth said as she pursued a passing tower of macarons.

"Beth . . . wait," I whispered, but she was already gone.

A part of me wanted to slink back and melt into the walls,

but I came here for answers. I stepped to the edge of the dance floor, to make myself known, when I spotted him across the room.

The moment our eyes met, my resolve seemed to seep right out of my pores. The way he maneuvered around the dancing couples was captivating, a dance unto itself, until all I could see was him . . . all I could hear was the sound of his footsteps beating in time with my heart. I wondered if he could hear it. I placed my hand over my chest to dampen the feeling, but the scar from our blood bond seemed to sear straight through to my palm. I forced myself to hold my breath for a moment. I wasn't sure what his scent would do to me.

He walked toward me, a hint of a smile tugging at the corner of his mouth, his eyes smoldering in the candlelight. Plucking a sprig of violets from one of the elaborate arrangements, he placed it in my hair. "Do you know what the violet symbolizes?"

"Death?" I replied.

He stepped closer, gazing down at me through his thick dark lashes, and I swore he could see right through me. Every fear, every nightmare, every drop of blood I spilled in his name. "It can also mean resurrection. It symbolizes fragility. A love taken too soon."

"Not soon enough." I removed the bloom from my hair, pulverizing it between my fingers.

On pure instinct, I breathed him in. His scent hit me like a powerful wave. I could taste him on the tip of my tongue. It was everything and nothing like I remembered. The sea salt riding on a hint of saddle leather. Sandalwood and musk mixed with mandarin. On paper, it would seem unharmonious, but here, in this moment, it was everything.

I glanced around the room, conscious of the gawkers looking for a juicy tidbit. "I can't do this . . . not here," I said as I turned to lead him out of the room, but he caught my hand.

"Dance with me." The warmth of his skin, the firm grip of his fingers took me aback. "I never got to dance with you at the meeting house. Watching you dance with Brennon was not my idea of a good time."

"Right. Wasn't that the night you tried to kill me in the corn? I mean, the *first* time you tried to kill me in the corn."

A few eavesdroppers looked on with wide eyes.

"Brilliant sense of humor, as always." He flashed an easy grin. "One dance." He led me to the dance floor, snaking his arm around my waist, his thumb resting precariously on my hip bone.

I stared down at his hand, hating myself for wanting to press into his touch, to feel his thumb singe a trail across my skin. "Don't even think about it," I said, raising his hand to my waist.

A slow smile eased across his lips. "I'm glad to see you remember."

In that moment I wanted to head-butt him in the face, make him bleed all over the pretty white tablecloths, but I restrained myself.

"See, I'm confused," I said, as he continued to waltz me around the room, flawlessly, I might add. "Who am I even talking to right now? Because the last time I saw you, you weren't *you*. You were Coronado."

"There was an adjustment period, to be sure, a delicate negotiation for control. But Coronado can be reasonable. It's me, Ashlyn. Blood and salt."

"How dare you say those words to me . . . my mother's words."

"But don't you see?" he whispered as he pulled me closer. "She was right. Those words belong to us. I carved out my heart and threw it into the deepest ocean. And I'd do it again and again. I will never be sorry for loving you."

"And what about lying to me, tricking me, killing all my ancestors?"

He took in a slow, deep inhalation, as if I'd just slipped a secreted dagger between his ribs. "You need to understand." He lowered his voice, a mist of remembrance coming over him. "I was groomed to do that. Your mother loved you, sacrificed herself so Katia couldn't have you, but my father sold me out from birth, practically threw me at Coronado to save his own skin. Ever since I can remember I was told that the Larkin vessel would bring the end of days. And I knew Katia's cruelty firsthand, that if she had her way, the world would live in her darkness. Delivering the Larkins to the corn was the only way to ensure there wouldn't be an heir. It was the only way to save humanity . . . to stop her. I truly believed that—that I was doing God's work."

I didn't know whether it was the movement, his scent, or his words, but I felt that I was spinning out of control. That I was falling right back under his charm.

"And then you came to Quivira," he said. "I remember thinking, how can something so beautiful be so evil? I loved you the moment I saw you. And maybe, initially, it was Coronado's blood in me, calling out for Katia's blood in you, but it went beyond that."

"Their love was sick and torturous."

"That may be true, but when their bond was severed, ours remained, stronger than ever. I've made mistakes, but haven't we suffered enough?" His breath grazed my neck. "We're like the dissonant chord in the finale of Beethoven's Ninth Symphony, begging for resolution. As long as we're apart, there will never be peace in the world . . . harmony."

"How do you know that piece of music so well?" I asked, struggling to keep ahold of my senses. "That's a long ways from the Backstreet Boys."

"We still have a lot to learn about each other." He stepped even closer, his lips skimming my ear. "But I know what makes you tick. I know the feel of your skin, how to touch you, what makes you quiver. I know how you taste, how you like to be kissed . . . how you *need* to be kissed."

With only a single weighted breath between us—just as I was on the verge of giving in—cameras began flashing around us.

The paparazzi. That's all I needed.

As if still in a daze, I pulled away from him and ran out of

41

the Rose Room, into the corridor. I didn't know what happened to me back there, but the more distance I put between us, the more I came back to my senses. I thought seeing him would bring answers, but it only brought more questions. It was Dane. I could feel him in every inch of my body, but there were things that didn't belong there. The fierceness of his jaw, the way the light caught his eyes, making them look more brown than blue. The way he spoke. It was Dane's voice, but the phrasing, the words, weren't always quite right. I wanted to know how it all worked—how Dane managed to gain control. And here I was, getting sucked in all over again. I was asking all the wrong questions. But this is what Dane did to me. He made me forget. But this wasn't about Dane or Coronado or even me anymore. This was about Rhys.

"Ashlyn, wait," Dane called after me.

Noticing the utility closet, the same one Rhys got stuck in years before, I seized the opportunity to do this away from prying eyes, and stepped inside, making sure to keep the door propped open a bit with my heel. Dane slipped in after me, but the space was smaller than I remembered.

I thought this would be easier in the dark, where I wouldn't have to look at his face, but the closeness only intensified the ache.

Before I could breathe him in again, I blurted, "Why the sudden interest in my brother?"

I felt something steel over him, like armor.

"For you," he answered, a little too late, stroking the ends of the ribbon tied around my wrist. I couldn't be sure, because there was only a sliver of light peeking through the door, but I swore I felt the silk coming to life, reaching out for his touch. "Finding him would be the greatest wedding gift I could offer you."

"Wedding gift?" And just like that, he threw me off point again. I pulled my wrist away. "Why have you been investigating the Wells, Perry, and Rhinebeck deaths?"

I sensed a shift in the ether. An infinitesimal crack in the veneer he was so desperately trying to present. "Curiosity. Same as you."

"You're hiding something. I can feel it."

He took in a deep breath, and when he exhaled, I felt the glacier begin to melt between us.

"You're right," he whispered. There was something almost intoxicating about the sadness pouring out of him. "I wanted to protect you, but it's gone too far."

"What are you talking about?"

He swallowed hard. "Rhys . . . he's in trouble."

"What kind of trouble?" I gripped his jacket, every possible scenario running through my head. "Tell me. Whatever it is. I can handle it. I just need to know."

"Your brother is responsible for the recent deaths."

"But how? We've been over the security footage. Rhys wasn't anywhere near—"

"Rhys and Spencer are working together."

"Spencer?" I balked. "As in your dad, Spencer?" I recalled my last memory of him, slitting my throat, leaving me for dead. "That's impossible. My brother would never team up with Spencer. And he'd never hurt anyone on purpose."

"Are you sure?" he asked, his eyes narrowing on me. "He was pretty angry at you . . . at me . . . at the world when he left Quivira. And we know how persuasive my father can be."

"I'm sure." I placed my hand on the door, preparing to leave. "So, if you have nothing else—"

"The men he killed . . . they were all immortals."

"What?" A chill ran through me, remembering how much Rhys hated the idea of immortality. "But how's that even possible?"

"His blood can kill any living thing, including immortals."

"So he can kill *you*," I said with a shaky breath. "That's why you're interested in him . . . why you're here now."

"No. I don't care about my own life—without you, I have no life—but we need to find him, before *they* do."

"They?"

"The council. The Arcanum, which I happen to be a member of."

"How many more of us are there?"

"There are twenty-five council members, but they're nothing like us. They're born of alchemy, with no ties to the spiritual world, and they can't blood bind. The centuries spent alone, without a connection like ours, have made them brutal to the core."

"But how would Rhys even know who they were?"

"We believe one of our own has betrayed us. Supplying them with resources, information, making it easy for them to pick us off. A play for power." He took a step closer. "The council won't stop until Rhys is buried a hundred feet below the ocean floor."

"Not if I find him first. I have my own—"

"Timmons," he interrupted. "And how's that been going for you?"

"We seem to be keeping up with you."

"I've *seen* Rhys, on surveillance footage."

"Where?" I took in a sharp inhalation of breath. "Where is he?"

"Valencia, Spain, was the last sighting, yesterday at the port. I believe he's on his way to me. The council will be arriving at my estate tomorrow to settle this once and for all."

"Settle this? I thought you were on my side, that you wanted to help find him before they do?"

"And we will. Keep your friends close, your enemies closer."

"I don't understand."

"I've convinced them that I have the key to finding and stopping the immortals' killer."

"And what would that be?"

"You."

I let out an uncomfortable laugh. "If these immortals are as ruthless as you say they are, why would they trust me? Rhys is my brother. My twin. They wouldn't believe that I'd allow him to be harmed."

"You're right. They wouldn't. But they would trust Katia to use her dark magic to find him . . . to bring him to justice."

"Okay, but Katia's dead."

"They don't know that."

"Wait, are you suggesting—"

"You look exactly like her. You were her intended vessel."

45

"No. Nope. No way." I started to leave when he grabbed my wrist.

"Please," he said, stroking his thumb against my pulse point.

I yanked my hand away, pressing my back against the door, not because I wanted to stay, but because I wasn't sure if my knees were strong enough to hold my weight.

"Just hear me out. No one knows Katia the way you do. The council fears her connection to the Dark Spirit. All we have to do is pretend for a little while, a few days tops."

"If you're a member of the council, why can't you just tell them that this isn't Rhys's fault—it's Spencer's. If we can find Rhys, I can talk to him, I can take him far away, where they wouldn't have to worry about him ever again—"

"That wouldn't be enough. These are the same people who ordered the Larkin killings. Coronado had no choice."

"What? I always saw Coronado as this heartless, powerful leader. I had no idea it was the council calling the shots all that time."

"There's a lot you don't know. And Coronado made his fair share of enemies on the council, and coming back with a new body—having to prove myself to them—well, I'm not exactly on their most-trusted list. I'm lucky to still have a position on the council at all."

"Lucky? So this is really about *you*—helping you get back in the council's good graces?"

"I want nothing to do with the council." I felt a flash of anger come over him. "They ruined my life. They used me to kill all of those innocent people. I can't let them kill Rhys, too."

A stab of pain hit me at the thought. "There has to be another way."

"Believe me. I wanted to shield you from what he's become. I know all too well what it's like to be betrayed by your own blood, but I've gone through every possible scenario and this is the only one where we control the information, we control the search, we control the outcome. Someone on the council is supplying Spencer and your brother with money, resources, names, and if we find out who that is, they could lead us straight to Rhys. But you have to understand the risk. If they ever found out the truth, about who you really are—that you're not Katia, that I'm not under Coronado's control—we'll both be in grave danger."

"We're immortal. What could they possibly do to us?"

I watched his Adam's apple depress. "That's something I hope you never have to find out."

The tone of his voice sent a chill racing up my spine.

"Come with me to Spain . . . tonight," he said as he pulled my hair forward, seductively arranging it over my shoulders.

And there was a part of me, the darkest part of me, that wanted to drop everything, leave with him this instant, but I needed to be smart about this. I wanted to make sure I was thinking with a clear head, and in order to do that I needed physical distance from him. There was no denying the effect he had over me . . . over my blood.

"I *will* protect you," he said, toying with the end of the black silk ribbon dangling from my wrist, "no matter the cost."

I drank in one last breath of him. "What if the only thing I need protection from is *you*?"

As I slipped out of the tiny space, the sound of the silk skimming across my skin did something to me, brought me right back to our final tryst under Heartbreak Tree, but I couldn't give in to this. It took everything I had to close the door behind me.

To walk away.

I knew it wouldn't take long for the Arcanum guards to free Dane, but it would be long enough to escape his scent, long enough to run from his blood, calling out for me like a siren song.

8

RUNNING OUTSIDE, DOWN the steps, I spilled onto Fifth Avenue, gulping down the putrid night air full of awful synthetic perfumes, sweat, kebab meat, and stale hot-dog water. I took it all in—anything to drown out his scent.

It wasn't until I reached the park, the safety of the trees, when I felt like I could breathe again.

"Ash, slow down. I can't run that fast." I heard Beth trailing after me.

"How did you—"

"Dane told me where to find you, said you needed me."

Reaching for the comfort of the ribbon, I panicked when I realized it must've fallen off somewhere, but I wasn't about to go back for it. Good riddance. "You can't help me, Beth. No one can help me. You should've stayed at the party. You don't want to be around me right now."

"Don't be silly. I belong with you. I told you that. Until the end."

A shiver of pain rushed through me. Suddenly, I knew what she meant. It wasn't until the end of my life, because that day would never come. It was until the end of *hers*. One day, I would be all alone, nothing but this ache in my bloodstream to keep me company. The thought was unbearable. I'd wasted a year of Beth's life, and for what? Rhys was still missing, on some immortal killing spree; I was crazier than ever; and Dane still had his hooks in me. I slumped to the ground under a massive oak.

Beth settled next to me, but didn't say a word.

"Rhys is in trouble," I finally admitted as I grabbed a rock, scratching a symbol in the earth. A circle with a cross in the middle. The alchemy symbol for chaos. "Dane told me Rhys has teamed up with Spencer. They're using his blood to kill immortals, and now the immortals are trying to kill him."

"Oh," Beth said, but she didn't seem that surprised.

"Dane said he can help me find him, if I come to Spain and pretend to be Katia, but there's something I don't understand. Dane has my blood. And I can *definitely* feel him. You have my blood, and I feel you. Rhys not only has my blood, but we're twins, for God's sake. Why can't I feel him? When I reach out for him . . . all I feel is . . . numb."

"Maybe that's how Rhys feels right now," Beth said softly. "Lost. I know what Spencer's like . . . what he did to Dane . . . to me. Who knows what kind of lies he's feeding him to make him do this. But if Dane says he can help, I believe him."

The dark feeling rose to the surface of my skin. I tried to

rub it from my arms, but it was no use. It felt like it was in my bones now.

"You don't trust him?"

"I don't know if I can trust anything about how I feel anymore," I said. "It's Dane. I could feel him in tiny gestures—the way he touched me, his posture, his gait—but there were other things that didn't feel quite right."

"You've been hurt before, but you can't let that stop you from experiencing love."

"Beth." I let out a deep sigh. "That's a line from the *Facts of Life* episode we watched last night."

"See, I told you Mrs. Garrett gives great advice."

"I don't think you get it. There was a moment when I asked him about Rhys, and his muscles tensed. And I knew he was hiding something from me. I called him on it and he came clean, said he was only trying to protect me." I clenched the rock in my fist. "But what if that's a lie, too? Fool me once, shame on you. Fool me twice, shame on me."

"Oh, that's good. That must be another Mrs. Garrett line."

"No, it's . . . never mind." I scraped away the symbol in the dirt. "It's deeper than getting my heart broken. Ever since Quivira, I've felt something simmering in me. A darkness. I don't know how to explain it, but seeing him did something to me. Awoke something in me. Whatever's inside of me, it feels like it wants us to be together."

"Like hormones?" Beth asked.

"Maybe. I don't know," I said as I threw the stone into the brush. "But being around him feels like a drug. And unfortunately, there's not a twelve-step program for 'I gave my sacred blood to a guy I'd known for seven days and now we're blood bound for all eternity.' I don't even know what to call him, Dane? Coronado?"

"Danado." Beth let out a gentle sigh.

"What?"

"That's how I like to think of him. He's a Dane and Coronado sandwich." She shrugged. "A Danado."

It started so small, a tiny tickle in the back of my throat. I tried to clamp down the feeling, but it spread through my head, my limbs, my chest. A lightness I hadn't felt in months. "*Dañado*?" I burst out laughing. "Do you know what that means in Spanish?"

"Does it mean hump-able?" she asked.

"No." I was laughing so hard, tears were streaming down my face. "It means 'damaged.'"

"I'm so sorry. I didn't mean—"

"No. It's perfect. It's absolutely perfect." The laughing died down, but the tears continued to flow.

As scattered and spacey as Beth was, I envied her. The way she saw the good in everything. "I wish I could give you my immortality. You'd use it to make a difference in the world. All I've done so far is amass a shit ton of gold and wallow in agony like some bitter spinster."

When Beth didn't reply, I glanced over to find her staring off into the distance, a hazy smile across her face, her palms held out in front of her. "It's snowing," she murmured.

"Beth? Are you okay?"

"But it's not cold," she said as she got up and started twirling around.

That's when I realized she was having a vision.

"And we're all together again. Like we were in Quivira."

"Where, Beth—where are we?"

"There's trees with silvery leaves and a big stone house."

"When?" I squeezed her shoulders. "When is this going to happen?"

She blinked hard, before focusing in on my face. "I don't know, but we're going to find him. We're all going to be together," she said with an excited giggle.

I grabbed her and hugged her tight. "I have no clue what you're talking about, but I'm so glad you're here. Thank you for coming with me, sticking by me all this time."

"You're stronger than your blood," she said, sending a chill across my skin.

"How did y—my mother used to say that."

"Oh, that makes sense." Beth shrugged. "She talks to me sometimes."

"Wait. What do you mean *talks* to you?"

"Most of the time she just tells me where to find wooden spoons and such."

It pained me to think of my mother in this moment, but maybe it was a sign. I'm the same girl who tracked her mother across the country. Survived a hostile takeover from a vengeful ancestor. I could make *gold*. Dane was immortal because of *me*. Because I chose to give it to him. The old Ash was still a part of me. Yes, there's loss and grief and heartache and despair and so much darkness, but there's also love and determination and faith. I have to believe we're going to find my brother. I have to believe that I can be around Dane without losing myself. I'm stronger than my blood. I have to be—for Rhys, for Beth, for myself, and for all the Larkin girls who've fallen before me.

I'm scared. But that's how I know I'm still alive inside.

Beth's backpack began to buzz. She opened it, revealing mounds of sweets she must've lifted from the party. Digging through cookies and cake, she pulled out her phone, answering it.

"Are you with Ash?" Timmons's frantic voice boomed. "Is she okay?"

"We're fine and dandy," Beth replied.

"Why is the connection so bad . . . where are you? I can barely hear you."

"Oh, it's frosting," Beth said as she licked it off the microphone. "Is that better?"

"Timmons?" I grabbed the phone.

"Ash, thank God. I just received a call from Dane Coronado, from *your* cell phone."

I checked my pockets and then I remembered the Arcanum guards had confiscated it. "Of course you did." I rolled my eyes.

"Everything he said checks out. I've looked into it and Spencer Mendoza is on the surveillance footage from the murders we've been tracking. He must be delivering Rhys's blood to the victims."

"We have to find Rhys before the other immortals do. The council—"

"Dane explained everything. He has a private plane waiting at the airport. Should I tell him we're on our way?" Timmons asked.

I took a deep breath. I didn't know if I could really trust Danado, but this was Rhys we were talking about. And Dane was my best shot at finding him right now.

"I'll go . . . I'll hear him out. But I'm not riding on a plane owned by the Arcanum. If I'm doing this, it has to be on my own terms. I'm calling the shots from now on."

9

BY THE TIME we landed in Barcelona, Beth had made friends with a sheik, a hairdresser from Milan, and a dog named Tinkles. The name was well deserved.

Timmons suggested we stop for some decent clothes before checking in. I glanced down at my bejeweled Times Square NYC airport sweatshirt. "I think I'm totally good with this."

"We look so cool." Beth beamed in her matching sweatshirt. "We're just like the Golden Girls."

"Didn't realize that's the look you were going for," Timmons said as he flagged a taxi.

The driver hopped out, a stocky man with a cap pulled down tight.

"Hotel Gòtic, please," Timmons told the driver.

Beth sat up front, chitchatting away with this guy, who clearly didn't speak much English. But she didn't seem to mind. And strangely enough, neither did he.

"I've taken care of everything, just as you specified. Dane assured me your conditions for the meeting will be met." Timmons pulled out a phone, showing me the itinerary. "You have a reservation at the Gòtic under your name and another room at La Terrassa under the name of Lucy Arnaz." He shook his head. "Really, Ash?"

I grinned. "That was Beth's contribution."

"You don't say." He sighed. "But I need you to take this seriously. The council is no joke. Coronado is the face of the Arcanum Corporation, but he's only a small cog in the machine. I'm still collecting intel, but I understand Coronado has been skating on very thin ice with the council, especially since his return from Quivira. There's talk of 'retiring' him."

"What does that even mean? He's immortal. What could they possibly do to him?"

"No idea, but it can't be good."

"If this is your idea of a pep talk, you're really shitty at it."

"Sorry. Just be careful, that's all I ask. As soon as you check in at the Gòtic, you and Beth can slip out the back and head for the other hotel." He swiped the screen. "Here's a map with the highlighted route. The restaurant is Les Quinze Nits. You should have a perfect view from your window. I'll be three blocks over at Café Leonre. If you need me for anything . . . anything at all. If he gets fresh with you or he—"

I squeezed his hand. "Thanks, Timmons." He was caught off guard by my sudden burst of affection, but it seemed to calm him down a little.

I'd been such an asshole to him, and still, here he was, going all the way across the world with me. It wasn't about the money. He was a Harvard graduate. He could get a job anywhere. And it wasn't just about my mother, either. He loved Rhys and he loved me. After this was all over, I needed to find a way to let him in. He was the closest thing to family we had left. And the last real connection to my mother. She'd want this. She'd want us to be close. I wasn't sure where Dane fit into this equation, but in Beth's vision, she saw us all together again, like we were in Quivira. Maybe it was possible.

I leaned my head against the glass, trying to hang on to a shred of the resolve I'd found in New York. I couldn't let myself go soft. Not now.

I wanted to believe Dane was helping me find Rhys out of the goodness of his heart, because God help him if this was just some pathetic ruse to save his own skin. I would slit his throat right there in that restaurant if I felt he was trying to manipulate me again. I'd love to see him try to explain how he healed right back up.

As we got closer to the city, it was impossible not to get caught up in the energy. There were blurs of red and blue motorbikes zipping by, clay-tiled roofs, and vibrant graffiti on buildings nestled together—a strange marriage of the old and the new.

I always thought Rhys and I would come here together. He was obsessed with the book *The Shadow of the Wind* our entire freshman year. Wouldn't shut up about it. I'd give anything to hear him rattle off those street names again.

"Look at that." Beth pointed up at a gorgeous church.

"L'església de Sant Jaume," the driver said.

We were getting close now. I tried not to get ahead of myself, but if Rhys was doing this as some twisted form of revenge, and Dane was his next target, he could be here right now. I closed my eyes, trying to reach out to him, to feel him, but the only thing I felt was Beth breathing on my face like a dehydrated dog.

"Wakey, wakey, Ashy. We're here."

Timmons placed the phone into my hand. "It's straight ahead. You can't miss it. I'll be waiting."

I gave him a curt nod, and we got out of the cab.

"And, Ash?" He called after me. "Nina would be very proud of you"

It took everything I had to hold myself together. I'd never wanted my mother so badly, for her to tell me this was the right thing to do—that I could handle this—but the only thing I felt was this darkness inside of me, pulling me forward. Pulling me toward him.

Swallowing the lump in my throat, I walked down a long shadowed alleyway that looked and smelled like it could've been from the fourteenth century. Beth followed at my side. A woman ducked out of one of the heavy arched doorways, dumping out a bucket of mop water. A man carrying huge baskets of flowers hurried past.

Had Katia taken this same path before? I knew she must've been in Spain around 1540 when she first got involved with Coronado. I always wondered whether they were born with a darkness in their hearts or whether it was the perfect storm: Two seemingly harmless elements coming together to form something deadly. Were they attracted to the darkness in each other? Did they bring it out in each other? Would they have always found the other in one form or another? I couldn't help but wonder if Dane and I were on the same path . . . if this was something inevitable. A broken circle, aching to be mended.

When we reached the end of the cobblestone path, it opened onto a vast, marble-tiled square. Plaça Sant Jaume. There was some kind of celebration going on with a live jazz band and swing dancers. On the other side of the square, people were crowded around a regal-looking building. City Hall. There were a half-dozen couples all decked out in suits and wedding dresses, waiting for their turn to get married. There were street kids running around, dodging the rose stands, singing and dancing for coins. It was like something straight out of one of those movies Beth liked to watch on TCM.

We wandered through the square, to a discreet black awning. The Gòtic Hotel. The doorman looked at us a little funny, probably wondering whether we were posh enough to stay there, but he opened the doors. We checked in and promptly went out the back entrance. I looked around to make sure we weren't being followed and pulled up the map. The layout of Barri Gòtic was nothing like the grid of New York City—the streets wind and stop, continuing on at a different point—it was complete chaos. "Whoever designed this city must've been drunk," I said as I studied the map.

"Why don't we just ask someone?" Beth chirped. "He looks nice." She started veering toward some sleazy-looking guy on the corner with way too much manscaping going on.

I pulled her back. "I've got this." We made a few wrong turns, but once I found the Ramblas, I got my bearings.

People walked so slow, I thought I was going to lose my mind, but I took a few deep breaths and looked ahead so I could chart our path through the clusters of tourists.

As soon as we emerged from the shady alleyways into the bright afternoon sun gracing Plaça Reial, it felt entirely different.

Swarms of seagulls, lovers strolling hand in hand, the smell of churros and chocolate, stirred something in me. It felt as if I'd been here before. In this exact same spot. Maybe in a dream or maybe Katia's memories were creeping in like poison. But even with the vibrant atmosphere, the warmth of the sun on my skin, the darkness pressed down on me. I knew Dane was close.

We checked into the second hotel with cash. No questions asked. They handed over a huge old key, attached to a giant block of worn, carved wood.

By the time we'd climbed the four flights of winding steps, we were both completely out of breath.

I started jiggering the key in the ancient lock, when an old man from next door peeked his head out.

I opened my mouth to say hello when he ducked back in, like a turtle going back into his shell.

"Okay . . ." I raised a brow.

The room was sparsely decorated. A rusted-out iron twin bed, with sheets so thin you could see right through them.

I pulled back the dusty drapes and peered down at the restaurant. It had an expansive outdoor terrace with the best view of the square. A place to see and be seen. I wanted this to be as public as possible. I wanted to make him squirm. Yes, I was on his turf, but I wanted him to know that I was in control.

One of my conditions was that I wanted to sit at an outdoor table, front and center. I didn't want to be boxed in, but here was the oddest thing. All the outdoor tables at our meeting place were empty, which didn't make any sense because there was a huge line of people waiting at the hostess stand. I looked around at the other restaurants around the plaza and all their outdoor tables were packed.

Beth sat on the bed, bouncing nervously. The springs were like something out of a nightmare.

"Stop. People are going to think—"

"What?" She stopped. "That we're having fun?"

"Never mind." I shook my head. "Just keep a lookout," I said as I headed to the bathroom. Turning on the ancient faucet, I splashed cold water over my face.

"He's here!" Beth hollered, making my heart leap into my throat. When I saw her opening the window, waving, I ran over, tackling her to the ground.

"We don't want him to know we're here."

"But aren't you supposed to meet him?"

"Please don't wave. Okay?"

"I'll try." She winced. "But it's hard."

I got off her and crawled back to the window. Dane wore a tailored black suit and a crisp white shirt, with signature Ray-Bans covering his eyes. He looked good. Too good.

Glancing down at my tacky sweatshirt, I was starting to have second thoughts. I didn't want him to think I was trying to impress him, but I didn't want to look hideous, either. After sniffing my armpits, I finally decided to peel it off, leaving me with a ratty black tank top. Better.

I watched four suited men enter the square and separate. I didn't need to see their marks to know they were Arcanum. They had that wolf-in-sheep's-clothing look. My instructions were to come alone, which he technically did, but he was already finding loopholes.

Dane glanced around the square, taking it all in before he approached the hostess stand. People were gawking at him, snapping pictures.

The hostess smiled up at him in a way that made my blood spike.

"Get ahold of yourself," I whispered to myself.

"I'm trying," Beth exclaimed. "I'm sitting on my hands!"

The hostess led him to one of the outdoor tables. Did he reserve the whole outdoor section of the restaurant? Wouldn't put it past him.

I took in one last cleansing breath. "Stay put," I said to Beth.

"This shouldn't take long. If anything happens, call Timmons."

Beth grabbed me, hugging me a little too long. "Don't do anything reckless."

As soon as I could, I broke away from her and rushed down the stairs, into the square.

I couldn't believe that I was here—that I was actually doing this.

But this wasn't about Dane or Coronado or even me. This was about Rhys.

I saw that Dane had taken a seat with his back facing the square.

Maybe it was because he didn't want to be photographed, but it gave me a minute to pull myself together.

"I'm stronger than my blood . . . I'm stronger than my blood," I whispered as I crossed the square.

But my blood wouldn't listen. The closer I got, the more I craved him.

My head was telling me to be cool, be cautious, but my heart, everything in my entire body, was screaming for something more.

10

MARCHING RIGHT PAST the hostess stand, I took the seat directly across from Dane.

"*Perdona'm.*" The pretty hostess rushed over. "This section is closed—I can find you another—"

"She's with me." Dane took off his sunglasses and looked across the square, waving, and like an idiot, Beth waved back from the open window.

I tried to match his smug expression, but it wasn't smug at all. He looked genuinely happy to see me . . . to see Beth. It caught me off guard.

"Perhaps, you'd like something to drink," he said. "Cava? Muscatel?"

"I'm only eighteen. Or in your case, five hundred and eighteen."

"Very funny. You're legal here."

"Really?" I replied, finding myself getting sucked into him all over again. "Look"—I sat up straight—"I didn't come here to drink with you."

The hostess stood there, clearly spellbound by Dane's presence.

"Water's fine," I said with a tight smile, just to give her something to do. "Don't you want anything?" I asked as I watched her skitter away.

"I never eat or drink in public places."

"Why? Afraid I'll slip something in your drink?"

He leaned forward, a little too close for comfort, but I didn't exactly pull away. "That's how your brother's blood is killing the immortals."

"Oh." I swallowed hard.

"You have nothing to fear, of course. Rhys's blood has no effect on you. We saw that in Quivira."

"And you also saw me save Beth from the effects of his blood. Is that why you're bringing me into this now? You think I'll open my veins to you again, save you if Rhys gets to you? Covering your bases?"

"I would never ask that of you."

"But you wouldn't exactly turn it down."

"I don't think you understand," he said with an intensity that caught me off guard. "Without your trust . . . your love . . . my life would be meaningless." He brushed a fingertip against the side of my knee, sending an electric current shooting through my bloodstream. "I'd gladly die if that's what you wanted."

I couldn't resist breathing him in, smelling the warmth from his skin, the sea salt, musk, and the mandarins.

"I'd hoped we could talk in private, but this was the best I could manage, given your demands."

The hostess put down my water, clumsily sloshing it over the sides onto the table, but she never took her eyes off Dane.

"Thanks," I said, a little too loud, to snap her out of it. "Does it ever get old?" I asked as I watched her swaying hips move away from the table. "The one-night stands. The womanizing."

A hint of a smile danced on his lips. "You must know, that's all for show."

"Please. I've seen you in all those magazines, with lots of girls. Beautiful girls. You're going to tell me you never—"

"Believe me, if I had, you'd know."

"I'm not that stupid," I said as I took a deep sip of water.

"I can prove it."

"How?"

He glanced up at the hostess, who appeared to be hovering at this point. "Close your eyes."

I took in a deep breath, wondering if I should trust him. But we were in a crowded square in the middle of the day—and I couldn't die—how could he possibly hurt me any more than he already had.

"Fine." I shrugged, closing my eyes.

"You'll know when to open them," he replied.

I heard him get up from his chair, the wrought iron scraping against cobblestones. He stepped away from the table, his scent trailing after him.

A murmur. A soft giggle. And then a twist of the knife, as if someone were hollowing out my chest. I felt a darkness spread over me, but it wasn't the same darkness I experienced over the past year. This was far more insidious, as if something were hacking away at my insides.

I opened my eyes to see Dane kissing the hostess, his hands gripping her waist.

"Dane," I called out for him in an involuntary gasp.

He released the girl; she staggered back, looking thoroughly stunned.

As soon as he walked back to me, the venom dissipated from my bloodstream, but the memory remained, like a stain on my heart.

"What just happened?" I asked, still trying to catch my breath.

"We're blood bound," he said, taking a seat. "If I'd been with another woman, you would've felt it," he said, glancing up at me seductively through his dark lashes.

"This isn't a game," I said as I shook my head. "I gave you immortality. Created you as my equal. But my equal would never lie to me, betray me . . . hurt me."

His smile dimmed, but the earnestness remained. "Then let me *prove* to be your equal."

I could feel regret, rising inside of him, or maybe it was

rising in me. In Quivira, my feelings for Dane were as simple as breathing. We were entwined in a lovers' knot I thought could never be undone. But now, it felt as if we were ensnared. A devil's knot of pain and remorse, guilt and shame. I didn't know how to move forward from this. To heal.

He reached for my hands, but I leaned back, as far away from his scent, his touch, as I could get. I had to keep sharp. "Before this conversation goes any further, I'm going to need to see that proof you told Timmons you had."

"Of course." He straightened in his chair, tentatively pulling a photo from his inside pocket, sliding it over to me. It was a grainy close-up shot of two people. One was Spencer; just seeing his face made my blood boil. The other one was a boy with sunglasses and a cap pulled down tight, but I'd know that nose anywhere, because it was the same as mine. It was Rhys.

"So it's true," I whispered. "Rhys must really hate me, what I've become, in order to do this."

"I'm so sorry, Ashlyn."

"When was this taken?" I turned the photo over and slid it back to him. I couldn't bear to look at the two of them together.

"Two days ago at the docks in Valencia. I have my best men on this, but the council is zeroing in. I've done my best to divert the information, but it will only be a matter of time before they find him."

A ripple of panic rushed through me. "But you said we could stop this."

"We can . . . we can save him if we work together."

I looked out over the crowd, trying to let everything sink in, but I didn't have time for that. Rhys didn't have time. "I'm not saying I'm agreeing, but if I did, how would we even do this?"

"I've persuaded the council to come to my estate. They arrive this evening. I told them Katia is the only person who can suss out this immortal killer."

"How? How would Katia even be able to do that?"

"Using her black magic. She's the only immortal who straddled both worlds—of alchemy and the spiritual. They fear her connection to the Dark Spirit."

I couldn't help wondering if that's what was happening to me—the darkness I've felt over the past year.

"What is it?" he asked.

I knew he could sense my fear, but I wasn't ready to name it.

"Nothing. It's just . . . what if we can't find him?"

"We will."

"Or what if we do? There's no way I'm handing over my brother."

"I've seen to that," he said as he leaned in. "I have a body," he whispered.

"A body?"

"We were able to procure a specimen matching your brother's description. When the time comes—"

"Wait! Is that even legal?"

"I can assure you he died of natural causes and the family was well paid—"

"Stop." I shuddered. "I don't want to know anything else about that."

"Good call."

"But how am I going to convince the council that I'm Katia? Have they met her? I don't have any powers. What if they want a demonstration?"

"Parlor tricks, nothing more," he said as he picked up the spoon and made it disappear. I remembered him doing that with the rose quartz in Quivira. "Coronado made it his mission to collect dirt on every single one of the council members."

"Of course he did."

"I feed you the information, and you can dazzle them with your dark intuition," he said as he made the spoon reappear, placing it on my nose.

The spoon slipped to the table with a loud clang.

"And they're just going to buy that Katia would be anywhere near Coronado without impaling him with a stalk of corn or whatever vegetable is lying around?"

"They had a complicated relationship, but it makes sense that they would reconcile in a time of crisis. Besides"—he leaned forward, oozing charm—"everyone knows, to resist a blood binding is pure torture. A sure way to madness."

"You know I won't sleep with you, right?"

"Don't be hasty." He smiled, the dimple on his right cheek peeking out as if to taunt me. "My bed comes from Switzerland, the finest goose down in all the world. It's really the most comfortable place to sleep, but you're welcome to your own quarters. I can be patient. We have all the time in the world."

"But my brother doesn't."

He looked down at the table, at the expanse between us, and I could feel his remorse . . . his humility.

"If you swear to find him, bring him back to me, *alive*, I'll do it."

He reached out to touch my face, I flinched at first—not because I didn't want him to touch me—I flinched because I wanted it more than anything in the entire world.

And he knew it.

11

TO MY SURPRISE, Dane didn't insist on accompanying me, but he did insist that I use his extra car and driver, which he just so happened to have on hand. More than a little presumptuous, but I didn't argue. I was tired of fighting him. Fighting myself.

After we parted ways, I walked across the square, halfway in a dream. I couldn't believe my brother was working with Spencer, but I saw the proof with my own eyes. Was he so angry with me that he wanted to kill every immortal? I felt like those people you always read about in the papers: family members of serial killers who had no clue. But Rhys wasn't just my brother. He was my twin. Did I somehow turn him into this?

As I trudged up the stairs to the dingy room, Beth was waiting on the landing, our backpacks at the ready.

"How did you—"

"Oh, I knew two days ago that we'd be going to his castle."

"Castle?"

"I'm excited to see it, you know, not just up in here," she said as she thumped her finger against her forehead.

After telling Dane's driver that we had a quick errand, we ditched our bags in the trunk of the car and went over a few cobblestone blocks to meet Timmons at a quaint hole-in-the-wall café, tucked away off a small square.

Timmons was hunched over his phone, his knee bouncing up and down like a jackhammer. That's when I noticed the empty espresso cups littering the table. He could never handle his caffeine. My mom used to tease him about it mercilessly.

As soon as we approached, he jumped up, practically knocking over the table.

"*Un altre?*" the waiter asked.

"Nope. I'm cutting you off," I said as I made him sit back down.

"Thank God, you're okay. I was worried sick," Timmons said as he perched on the edge of his seat. "I've been doing some digging into the council, and it's worse than I thought. There are heads of state—royalty—captains of industry—these people are not to be tangled with. And as far as the council is concerned, there is no Dane. It's only Coronado in Dane's body . . . and they hate him."

"So I've gathered."

"You know how there was talk of retiring him—well, apparently, there've been several members over the years who have fallen out of favor with the council and they've just disappeared. Poof. Never to be heard from again. Oh, and it gets better." He took in a shallow breath. "Rumor has already spread throughout the community that Katia is coming back; he went ahead and told them you were coming before you even agreed. You don't find that troubling?"

"Dane knows I would do anything to find my brother."

"And then what?"

"Well, Dane has a body on hand—"

"Of course he does. Body or not, do you really think they're just going to let you go? The most powerful witch in the world? They have every resource at their disposal. They'll find you."

"But that's where you come in." I patted his hand. "No one can hide money and assets better than you. We're going to need an exit plan."

"You're basically doing this to keep me busy, aren't you?"

"Possibly. But you're right. We need to prepare for every scenario."

"I'm assuming Dane told you that, in exchange for your services, the council has agreed to release Dane to you. Is that how he got you to agree to this? Emotional manipulation?"

"No," I whispered, replaying our conversation in my head. "He didn't mention anything like that. Are you sure?"

"Dead sure. My source said they've been trying to get rid of Coronado for decades, but his connection to you is the only thing that's kept him around. Forgive my Spanish," he said as he looked at his notes. "*Besat per la foscor.* 'Kissed by darkness.'"

A shiver of recognition pulsed through my blood. Why wouldn't he have told me that?

"Did he also neglect to mention that the three dead council members voted to retire Coronado early, with or without Katia's consent?"

"What are you trying to say?"

"There are a lot of moving parts here. How do you know you can trust him? After everything he's done to you and your family? Dane or Coronado . . . or whatever he is."

"Danado," Beth and I answered in unison.

He gave us a weirded-out look, but continued. "Funny how he seemed to do perfectly fine without you for the past year. It's only now, when his life is in real danger, that he reached out. Maybe Rhys has his reasons . . . maybe Danado deserves to die."

"Timmons," Beth shushed him.

"It's okay, Beth," I said as I pushed the sugar bowl over to her to calm her down. "It's a valid question. Are there glimpses of Coronado in there? The cockiness . . . for sure. Do I know exactly what I'm dealing with? No. But Dane and Coronado both know how much Rhys means to me. They owe me this. If pretending to be Katia can throw the council off the trail long enough for Dane and me to find Rhys first, it's worth it."

Timmons gave me a look.

"I get your concern, I really do. But I can handle him this time. *I've* changed. Besides, I'll have Beth."

We looked over at Beth, who was staring off into space as she poured sugar packets onto her outstretched tongue.

"Yes. That's a real comfort," Timmons said. He looked around before tucking a small phone under his napkin and sliding it over to me. "It's a burner. Untraceable. Keep it hidden. You need to check in with me every day. If something happens and I don't hear from you . . . Well, I know I can't kill them, but I can cause a hell of a scene."

"Got it," I said as I slipped the phone into my pocket.

"As your lawyer, I'm telling you to run; as your friend, I'm telling you to watch your back."

12

AS BETH AND I said our good-byes and walked back toward the waiting car, I noticed an old apothecary shop at the end of a narrow alleyway. It reminded me of something out of *Romeo and Juliet*. A man stepped out from behind the counter and came to the doorway, giving me a slight bow.

He was probably in his twenties, handsome, immaculately dressed. But there was something very Old World about him. I took in a deep breath and had a flash, nothing more than a split second—like a blinding burst of sunlight peeking through passing skyscrapers—where I saw him standing in that same spot, dressed in tails and a top hat, waiting for someone. Waiting for me.

"Do you know him?" Beth asked.

"I'm not sure."

As I took a hesitant step toward him, he slipped inside as if he wanted me to follow, which I did.

"Ash, I'm not really sure if we have time for—"

I knew she was right, but the moment I entered the shop, I felt something open inside of me. Like taking that first deep hit of air after you've been released from under a riptide.

The shop was full of the regular things you might see in a forgotten pharmacy—dusty aspirin, bandages, sun lotion—but beyond that there were pestles, herbs, oils, and a sheen of fine gold dust clinging to the grooves of the worktables. He was an alchemist. And, I'd gather, an old one at that. Definitely immortal. I could smell the centuries on him.

Following his scent of cypress, brisk granite, and black sage, I gravitated toward the back of the room. Behind a heavy tapestried curtain was a small inner chamber, adorned with art and antiques, layers of Persian rugs, and an old record player, Mozart lilting through the cozy space.

"May I read for you?" he asked as he took a seat behind a claw-foot mahogany table, fanning a deck of cards before me. The backs of the cards were the color of wet shale with a handpainted ouroboros symbol, the snake eating its own tail, each scale gilded with painstaking care.

"Sure, I'll bite," I said as I stepped up to the table.

He pursed his lips as if he were stifling a smile.

"Choose three."

I reached to grab the first one in front of me.

"No, not like that." He took my hand, fanning out my fingers. "Skim your fingertips over every card, and let your soul choose for you."

79

I did as he said. I felt silly at first, but soon I relaxed, letting my senses lead me to the first card. I swore I could feel the energy thrumming through my palm. "You're immortal," I said, dragging the first card forward.

A mischievous smile crept into the corner of his mouth. "What gave me away? My boyish good looks or the smell of my blood?"

I looked up at him sharply.

"All immortals have a heightened sense of smell, but yours is especially keen."

Interesting. So he could smell it on me, as well. Time to test the waters.

"I'm Katia, but you probably already know that," I said as I slid another card from the spread.

"Rennert, the alchemist, at your service."

"Are you part of the council?" I asked, searching for another card.

"I prefer to remain on the fringe. But certain members of the council seek me out when they are in need of my skills."

"And what are those?" I asked, sliding the final card forward from the deck.

"All sorts of follies and unpleasantries. But I wouldn't be in business very long if I spilled my secrets so easily."

"Are you a seer?" I asked.

"Heavens, no." Rennert crinkled up his nose as if he were disgusted by the notion. "No offense," he said to Beth.

Beth tugged on the edge of my shirt even harder. "Ash, I really think we should—"

"Your past," he said, placing his hand on the first card, but not turning it over. "There's a tree, split down the middle, roots reaching through your bloodline. There's pleasure and pain, passion and death—so much death—but there's also love. Deep sacrifices have been made for this to come to pass."

Beth laced her cold fingers through mine. She was scared.

"Your present," he said, caressing his thumb over the second card. "Danger abounds." He looked at me with a raised brow. "There's a battle between your heart and your mind. Judgment and forgiveness. You're standing on the precipice, a razor's edge. It's all so delicious," he said, a grin easing across his lips. "Do you let yourself fall once again or do you hold on to the guilt and bitterness that have become your constant companions? To dance with the darkness. To dance with the light. Which will you choose?"

I stared down at the third card, sensing the weight of it and everything it implied.

"Your future." As soon as he placed his hand over the last card, I watched the tendons in his hand flare, the tension traveling up his arm, like visible poison. "Twins. All coiled up. Vessels for each other."

"Rhys," I whispered.

"The light you carry inside you was a gift, but it's not meant for you. It's keeping the darkness at bay, but if you hold on to it, it will be your ruin. In order to save yourself, to save them all, you'll have to give it away and step fully into the darkness. The darkness may be your curse, your immurement, where your heart will turn to ash . . . but it's your only chance at salvation. Remember, no one is irredeemable, Ashlyn."

"H-how did you know my name? How did you know my mother used to say that?"

"I knew Katia. Who do you think made her immortal?" His head snapped toward the windows, a look of unease coming over him. "The reading is over. Now, if you'll excuse me, I have important matters to—"

"What did you mean about the twins? The vessel? Did you see my brother?"

"Good day," he said, turning his back on me.

"Am I becoming like Katia . . . is that what you're trying to tell me?" When he didn't answer, I frantically flipped over the cards to find they were blank—and so was the entire deck.

Beth yanked on my shirt to leave, but I didn't need any more encouragement. I was thoroughly creeped out.

Just as we were almost to the door, he turned toward me. "Ashlyn, wait. You have a light of your own. Trust your blood. Trust your instincts. And don't worry, I will keep your secret until my dying breath," he said with a sweet sadness. "Now go."

I hadn't taken two steps away from the shop when a man in a smart seersucker suit and a straw hat hurried by, brushing up against my shoulder. He was drenched in a terrible amber cologne that couldn't mask the fact that he was an immortal, too. He glanced back at me as if he could feel what I was. As soon as our eyes met, he tilted his hat to obscure his face and slipped inside the shop, locking the door behind him.

13

WANTING TO PUT as much distance as she could between us and the mysterious alchemist, Beth pulled me toward the awaiting car. She didn't say anything, but I knew she was spooked by the encounter. Maybe it was a seer thing. I didn't know what his story was, but he certainly knew a great deal about me. And Katia. More than I was comfortable with. But for some reason, I trusted him.

As Beth and I climbed into the back of a luxurious car, the driver watched us from the rearview mirror. He was a stern-looking man with the telltale mark of the Arcanum on his wrist. I tried not to think about the guards marching into the corn with Coronado last summer, Katia using her dark magic to kill them all. And now here I was, in Spain, under their protection. The irony wasn't lost on me.

As we pulled away, I couldn't stop thinking about what Timmons said, warning me about Dane, how it was telling that Dane hadn't tried to contact me until his life was in danger.

But then I remembered Beth's vision of the four of us standing together under a warm but snowy sky. I didn't know what it meant—and Beth probably didn't, either—but the bottom line was that Rhys and I would be together again. And Dane and Beth would be a part of that. As long as they were with me, it could happen at any time.

It was Timmons's job to be cautious, but I was pretty sure Dane didn't have it in him to betray me again. At least I didn't think so.

"Beth, if there's anything you need to tell me," I said as I settled back into the seat, "anything I should know, now would be the time." But when I looked over, she was out cold.

"Sugar crash," I murmured.

We went through a tunnel, the lights flickering inside the car like a rave.

I was exhausted, but the adrenaline pumping through me wouldn't let me rest. As we emerged from the tunnel, I counted the palm trees. I didn't even know Spain had palm trees. So far, this trip was full of surprises. Dane showing his vulnerability being the biggest one of all. Seeing him. Feeling him, as if we'd never been apart.

The farther we drove south along the coastline, the more disjointed I became. Maybe it was the lack of sleep, the alchemist's words, but the only reminders of modern times were from the power lines crisscrossing the countryside or the occasional defiant swath of graffiti splattered over ruins. There were medieval villages carved into the hillsides, where even the hills seemed to have a life of their own. Colors of salmon, saffron, and greens—deeper than sage, lighter than moss. There was dense vegetation, abandoned sunflower fields, and tall slender trees, sticking up like needles. Everything felt rich and old—with a layer of dust falling over the Moorish architecture, making it look like an old hazy photograph.

A few hours had gone by when we pulled off the main road, passing through a small village. Cathedral bells were tolling, but it wasn't Sunday. Men tipped their hats, women curtsied as we drove by. It made me wonder if they knew about Coronado and his young heir. If they knew about me. I was probably just being paranoid. Rhys would've told me I was being a total narcissist, but I couldn't shake the feeling that they knew my face. That they were expecting me.

14

WE PULLED UP to a massive set of black iron gates. Security cameras were everywhere. It looked more like a military checkpoint than the entrance to a home. But when a flood of black birds flew overhead, I knew this was it. Castell de Coronado.

One of the Arcanum guards stepped forward, opening my door.

"Why are we stopping here?" I asked.

"Protocol. No vehicles are allowed beyond the gates."

At first I thought it was stupid, but then I remembered a very similar scene from one of the Godfather movies. Not that I wouldn't survive a car bomb, but that could get messy.

I reached over to wake up Beth, when she sat up with a gasp. "He's here."

"What?" I asked. "Who?"

I looked up to see Dane strolling down the drive. In the hazy glow of the late afternoon sun, he looked like something out of a dream.

As soon as I stepped out of the car, the scent of sea salt, mandarins, and cypress trees washed over me. But there were other scents, too. Metal, gunpowder, mercury, bleach, and iodine.

As the men took our bags, Beth gripped the car door, a faraway look coming over her.

"What is it?"

"Octopus," she replied.

"Octopus? Is that some kind of code for something?"

"No. That's what they had for lunch."

"Great." I let out a deep sigh. Glad to know her seer skills were coming into good use.

"Welcome home, Katia," Dane said as he greeted us at the gate.

Just hearing her name escape his lips set something off inside of me. It was the way he said it, how easily it rolled off his tongue.

"This is only temporary," I said as I slammed the door shut. "Just until we find Rhys."

"Or maybe you'll never want to leave," he said as he arranged a tendril of my hair over my shoulder.

The dark feeling welled inside of me, making me short of breath.

As much as it pained me to admit it, he was just as arresting as he was on the first day we met. Maybe even more. The Dane I knew in Quivira had an edge about him, but this Dane was relaxed. I started to reach out to get a sense of his emotions, but stopped myself. I needed to keep a healthy distance.

I pulled my hair back, away from his touch, and continued

walking. The ground crunched beneath my boots, but it wasn't gravel . . . it was shells. The sea was close; I could smell the brine, taste it in the breeze.

Beth lagged behind. She still seemed to be half asleep, or maybe it was all an act to give Dane and me a moment alone.

As we crested the hill, the castle came into full view. I stopped so I could take it all in. It was far from the cold medieval fortress I was expecting. There was a huge main building with a breezeway connecting a tower on each side, and dozens of charming stone structures spread around the outskirts of the main property. It was breathtaking. Begonias and ivy climbed the soft gray stone; there were lush gardens and manicured hedges. And as far as the eye could see, there were rows and rows of trees with silvery leaves, exactly like the ones Beth described in her vision. The realization filled me with a surge of hope.

I studied him as he spoke and for the first time I thought maybe it was possible—that he and Coronado could be coexisting peacefully in the same body. I wanted to ask him how it all worked, but that's not why I came. I was there for Rhys. I needed to remember that.

"So, what's our backstory?" I asked, forcing myself to look away from his perfect mouth. "Last time I checked, Katia hated your guts. She would've basically done anything to eat your face for breakfast."

He cracked a lopsided grin. "It's simple, really. I asked for your help, and you came."

"And what's in it for Katia?" I prodded.

"Other than all this?" he said as he panned his hand down his body.

"I'm serious." I slapped him in the chest, trying not to think of how firm his muscles were. "Katia would never agree to do something like this out of the goodness of her heart."

"True." He dragged his hand through his hair. "Katia and the council have been at war for centuries. You find the immortal killer for them, and all will be forgiven. We'll be free to live our lives."

I wasn't sure why he wasn't telling me the truth—that a deal had been struck for his safety—but I had bigger worries at the moment.

"I need to know exactly what I'm walking into."

"This holds all the information I was telling you about. Everything you need to know," he said as he handed me a small, leather-bound notebook. It was warm from his body heat—from his skin. As much as I wanted to smell it, I resisted, placing it in my back pocket. "Who you've met, your shared memories, plus a little extra. There's enough dirt in there on every council member to not only make them believe you're Katia, but to believe you can get into their heads. After tonight, they'll keep their distance."

"Not the most subtle approach."

"Katia wasn't known for subtlety," Dane said. "Study it. Memorize it. If you get stuck, lean on me, reach out for me, and I'll do my best to steer you along."

The thought caught me off guard. I'd worked so hard to build a dam between us, but the idea of letting go, using my senses to reach out for him, to feel what he was feeling, brought a flutter of excitement to my blood. I had to be careful. I knew how intoxicating that could be. And I couldn't afford to lose myself . . . not again.

"Fine, I creep them out, but how is that going to help us find Rhys?"

"Once they trust you, trust your powers, all it will take is a few misdirected leads to buy us some time. I brought them here so we could control every aspect of the hunt. I have my best men working around the clock on this. We're closing in on Rhys and Spencer. I can feel it. But tonight is all about convincing them you're Katia. And if we agitate a few people in the process, it might lead us to the traitor who's supplying means and information to Rhys and Spencer. Maybe we can take care of this quietly before anyone gets hurt."

"And if that doesn't happen?"

"Tomorrow morning there will be an official meeting. There, I will present everything we've gathered; of course I'll leave out the key details. No matter what's said at that meeting, you need to remember that I'm on your side. I will bring Rhys back to you, safe and sound. That is my promise. And later, over a leisurely lunch, the two of us will come up with a plan of our own."

"You mean the three of us," I said as I glanced back at Beth, who appeared to be off in her own little world, talking to herself.

"Of course. Beth is a part of our family. But while the council is staying on the estate, she'll need to keep hidden. For her own safety. For just a few days."

I wanted to argue with him, but then the staff began to file out of the castle onto the massive stone steps, all in crisp black-and-white uniforms.

A statuesque woman in a body-hugging but prim black dress approached. Her only adornments were a worn silver amulet on a chain around her neck and a leather belt cinched around her tiny wasp waist, with a set of old-fashioned keys dangling from it. She moved like a cat, fluid but powerful, every muscle used with purpose. A frightening show of restraint.

"This is Lucinda," Dane introduced me.

She looked me over, her eyes searing across my skin. She was beautiful, but severe looking. Olive skin, piercing dark eyes, and eyebrows to match. Oxblood-colored lipstick accentuating the hard line of her mouth. There was something so familiar about her—arresting. I couldn't take my eyes off her.

"Lucinda will show you to your quarters. She runs things around here."

"But—"

He pulled me in to him, whispering in my ear, "I trust Lucinda with my life. She's the one who transcribed Coronado's memories of Katia and the council members for me. You're going to have to trust me on this one."

I whispered back, "The last time a pretty boy said that to me, I ended up naked under a willow tree, giving him my immortal blood."

"I may be pretty, but I'm no boy," he said as he stepped away, dragging his thumb across my hip bone.

"Come," Lucinda said, in a strong Spanish accent. Gripping my elbow, she led me past the staff and into the main hall, which was nothing short of astounding. The floor in itself was a work of art: a stunning mosaic of blues, deep reds, and greens that depicted Coronado's signet. The vaulted ceilings were painted in a breathtaking fresco. The scent of old parchment, oiled leather, and freshly burned cedar lingered in the air.

As we walked past a stately library on my left-hand side, toward the grand staircase I caught my reflection—only it wasn't *my* reflection.

I pulled away from Lucinda and doubled back, peering at a huge portrait hanging above the fireplace. My eyes. My mouth. But the woman in the portrait had a confidence I'd never possessed. She was in a state of undress, with a deep blue silk gown draped precariously around her hips, glancing seductively over her shoulder. "Katia," I whispered.

"Francisco commissioned this in 1610 from the artist Peter Paul Rubens," Lucinda said, startling me. "Even after more than fifty years of your absence, Coronado was able to convey your likeness." She stared at the painting as if it were a living, breathing thing, something she despised to the core. "All the way down to the corners of your pretty mouth." Her words felt like an assault, as if she were hacking away at my face with every syllable. "And now you're back." She attempted a smile, which was almost more frightening.

A strange sound echoed over the marble foyer, as if someone were pouring a pitcher of water onto the floor.

Looking down the main hall, I found Beth standing perfectly still, facing a wall, as she urinated on the floor.

"Beth." I hurried over, easing my hand onto her shoulder, but she just stood there, as if in a trance. "What is it?" I asked as I inspected the wall, but there was nothing there. "Do you see something?"

Lucinda snapped her fingers at the staff and they hopped to. "I wish you would have told me your mortal isn't house-trained."

"My mortal?" I looked at her in confusion. "Something must've spooked her is all." But I'd never seen Beth react this strongly to anything.

"It's a vortex," Beth murmured. "This entire place is a vortex of pain and death, just like the sacred circle in Quivira."

Maids descended on us, mopping up the floor between Beth's legs.

"What are you talking about? Are you okay?" I asked as I pulled her away from the puddle. She blinked hard, a single tear trailing down her cheek. "I'm not sure. Maybe it's the jet sag."

I didn't bother correcting her. "I'm feeling the jet sag, too," I said as I put my arm around her and led her back toward the staircase.

As Lucinda led us up two floors, she went over the ground rules. "Under no circumstances will your mortal be allowed to roam the castle while our guests are present."

I hated the way she talked about her, like she was my pet. "Her name is Beth, and what if she's hungry? What if she's bored?"

"Mr. Coronado has seen to everything. We have been informed that her safety is our highest priority."

I helped Beth up another winding staircase, this one made from ancient stone, to find two Arcanum guards stationed in front of a heavy iron door.

Lucinda nodded curtly, and they stepped out of the way with military precision.

Unlatching the key ring from her belt, Lucinda opened the door to an enormous suite filled with books, food, and drink. There was a giant canopied bed in the middle, fit for a princess.

I stepped inside and approached a tray on the sideboard. I held up a tiny triangle sandwich and showed it to Beth. "Cucumber. And there's a pitcher of lemonade muddled with strawberries. All your favorites."

"It's lovely," Beth murmured as she stared out of barred windows that crawled with begonias.

"Come," Lucinda said as she marched Beth to the bathroom, turning on the shower and ordering her in.

As soon as Beth took off her clothes and stepped in, Lucinda picked them up with a pair of ice tongs, placing them in a garbage bag. "Savages," she muttered as she fetched a nightgown and robe from the dresser, setting them on a damask-covered bench in the bathroom.

"Look, that's never happened before. She's normally extremely potty trained—wait . . . why am I even explaining this to you?"

Lucinda stuck her hand in the shower, turned it off, and gruffly handed Beth a towel.

Beth stepped out, and I helped towel her dry, then got her into the nightgown and robe. "Don't listen to her," I assured her. "It was an accident."

"Come," Lucinda barked, making us both flinch.

"I think she might be getting sick," I said as I led her into the bedroom. "Maybe we should call a doctor—"

"No." Beth gripped my arm. "No medical equipment. No needles. No doctors."

"Why? What's going on?"

"It's nothing. I'm fine," she said as she crawled under the covers.

I sat next to her. "Are you sure you're okay with this? We can leave right now if—"

"No." She reached for my hand. Her skin was cold. "This is where we need to be. I'm just tired."

I'd never seen her this worn-out before, but I'd never flown to another country with her, either.

"She'll want for nothing," Lucinda said. "I'll see to it personally."

Lucinda wasn't the warmest caregiver, but Dane said he trusted her with his life. That should count for something.

I turned my attention back to Beth. "I'll come and check on you as soon as I can," I said, brushing the hair away from her forehead.

"We're going to find him," Beth whispered. "It's almost like he's already here with us. It won't be long."

Lucinda tapped her designer heel on the slate floor. I looked up to find her glaring down at me and I wondered if this was a small preview of what I was about to walk into tonight—a den of vipers.

As they closed the iron door, I watched Beth pull the covers up under her chin, a haunted look on her face as she gave me one last wave.

15

LUCINDA POWER WALKED down the stone steps to a long corridor, through a dizzying breezeway that connected the tower, leading to another enormous corridor. There were only two doors on the entire floor.

"This is the oldest part of the castle, the original master's quarters. Of course, Mr. Coronado made some adjustments over the past year, in anticipation of your arrival."

She used one of the ornate iron keys to open the first door. I stepped inside. It was like walking into a dream. A gorgeous mahogany sleigh bed with sumptuous linens, windows opening up to a formal garden, and, beyond it, the sea. Marble inlaid floors covered in hide rugs, a massive fireplace, and rugged stone walls.

"Where does this lead?" I pressed my palm against a door next to the bed.

"To Francisco's chamber—I mean, Dane's," she corrected

herself. "Mr. Coronado said that you are the only one to have a key to this door," she said as she removed it from her key ring and handed it over.

As curious as I was to see Dane's room, I tugged on the doorknob to make sure it was secure, then placed the key in an elegant agate box on the bedside table.

Fetching a robe from the closet, she placed it on the bed. "You will need to get washed and changed. I'll start the bath—"

"No," I said a little too forcefully, remembering my creepy welcome party in Quivira, but then quickly dialed it back. "Thank you, but I can bathe myself. Been down that road. Not gonna happen."

"Americans," she muttered as she started to leave.

"My bag?" I asked.

"By the time you get out, you'll have everything you need."

As soon as she left, I locked the door and looked for a place to stash the phone Timmons gave me. I knew Dane said he trusted Lucinda with his life, but I was getting a completely different vibe from her. Sort of an I'd-like-to-kill-you-with-my-death-stare vibe. Under the mattress: way too obvious. I looked under the rugs for a loose tile, but this place was impeccably maintained. I was going to have to get creative.

I went into the bathroom to look for a hiding spot. I was shocked to find it fully stocked with every beauty product under the sun. Makeup, hair supplies, lotions, face creams, powders, but no perfume. He remembered that I didn't wear perfume.

I grabbed a plastic shower cap and wrapped the phone, then submerged it in a jar of body cream.

Beth would be so proud. This was straight-up MacGyver-level sneaky.

I turned on the faucets of the pink tub, then realized that it wasn't just pink—it was made from a solid piece of rose quartz. I'd never seen anything like it.

After pinning up my hair, I went back in the bedroom, stripped off my clothes, put on the robe, and grabbed the notebook Dane gave me.

"I have to hand it to Mr. Coronado," I said as I submerged myself in the steamy water. "He seems to have thought of everything."

The notebook was full of names with thumbnail photos attached. Histories full of devious deeds. Slave traders. Blood diamonds. Aristocrats and thieves. But there was nothing on Lucinda. I wondered what her deal was. She was old and full of secrets. I could smell it on her. But who was I to judge? We all have things we need to hide.

Just as I was rinsing the soap from my shoulders, I heard the lock to my door unlatch, followed by a flurry of footsteps.

"Excuse me," I called out. "The door was locked for a reason."

"Calm yourself," Lucinda scolded. "We are only dropping off your things."

I heard the rattling of wood, a match being struck, the pop of a cork, followed by retreating footsteps. All but one set.

Lucinda. I could smell her—beneath her heady, ancient blood and the freesia lotion she used, there was a sharp disinfectant smell tinged with iron—and she was standing directly in front of the bathroom door.

I gripped the loofah brush in my hand. "If you even think about coming in here, there will be blood."

"Don't tempt me," she muttered. "Our guests will be arriving in an hour. Mr. Coronado's very anxious to see which gown you'll choose."

"Gown?" I leapt out of the tub. "Hey, wait a minute." I grabbed a towel. "I didn't bring a gown."

I raced out of the bathroom, to the door, peeking my head out into the corridor, but Lucinda was already gone.

I looked over the room, now transformed by flowers and firelight. The scent was captivating—honeysuckle, peonies, and violets, cedarwood burning in the fireplace, along with the smooth notes of ripe fruit from the bubbly that was nestled in a silver ice bucket.

It was a bottle of cava. A glass had been poured, and there was a note propped against it.

Dane's handwriting. I'd recognize it anywhere.

The pain of finding that letter under Heartbreak Tree came back to me in a searing flash as I ran my fingers over the script.

> *The choice is yours.*
> *I will follow your lead.*

> *All my love,*
> *Dane*

I stared at the two garment bags draped on my bed. Afraid to open them. Afraid not to.

I unzipped the black garment bag first. It was a beautiful gown, similar in color to the one Katia was *sort of* wearing in the portrait. Midnight-blue lace and silk, with a sheer but demure high neckline and delicate cap sleeves, but the back . . . well, there was no back. It was like somebody forgot to sew on half the dress.

"Nice try," I said, laying it down on the bed.

But when I unzipped the white bag, my blood turned cold.

It was a wedding dress. Absolutely stunning, but no fucking way.

I wadded it up, cramming it into the bottom of the armoire. I didn't even want to look at it.

And it appeared that Morticia Addams had already taken away the clothes I came in with, probably buried them along with my bag from the car.

I had half a mind to go down there naked. That would serve him right, but I'd only be hurting myself.

As irritated as I was, I needed to be smart about this. Not only for Rhys's sake, but also for Dane's. Timmons said that if he didn't deliver me, they were going to "retire" him, whatever that meant. I couldn't let that happen. No. I needed to play my part to perfection: the ruthless immortal who stole Coronado's heart.

Holding the deep blue gown in front of me, I looked in the mirror. "If they want a villain, I'll give them a villain."

16

WHEN I FINALLY worked up the nerve to leave my room, I noticed how quiet the house felt. Too quiet for a party. The only sound was the click of my heels, followed by the silk of my dress swishing against the marble floors. As I descended the staircase, I found the staff bustling with overflowing trays of food and drink.

"Don't mind if I do," I said as I snatched a glass of bubbly off one of the passing trays and followed the server to the back of the house.

Beyond the open French doors, the formal garden, and the gorgeous black-bottomed pool was a huge expanse of grass, with at least a couple dozen people standing around in tuxes and gowns. To be more specific, twenty-five immortals who were hell-bent on killing my brother. Some I recognized from newspapers, magazines, CNN. The top one percent of the one percent. And now I had to pretend to be one of them.

I wanted to run back upstairs and hyperventilate for a while, but my heels were stuck in the soil.

"You're late," said Lucinda, who'd snuck up behind me.

"Jesus." I flinched. "You might want to consider wearing a bell."

"I hope you realize how lucky you are to be welcomed here, after everything you've done to him."

"To *him*?" I let out an uncomfortable laugh, but when I looked over at her, I felt the heat of her emotions—longing, pain, devotion, pure jealousy—smoldering behind her golden-hazel eyes.

"Luckiest girl in the world," I said as I slipped off my heels and handed them to her.

"And what am I to do with these?" she asked, her dark eyebrows knitting into a thin grim line.

"I'm sure you'll find a place to stick them," I said before stepping forward.

The grass felt good between my toes—it wasn't Quivira grass, but it felt right.

As I moved through the crowd, I let myself remember what it was like to have Katia's power running through my bloodstream. I needed to channel her strength, her confidence to get through this.

I sensed eyes on me as I passed—their judgment, hate, and fear trying to penetrate my skin.

Maybe it was just the cava or the jet sag, but I swore I felt something . . . a darkness reaching up through the soil, taking root in my body.

I couldn't get the alchemist's words out of my head. What would make me give away my light and succumb to the darkness? What would drive me to burn down the world and bathe in its ashes? Not wanting to give in to my fear and paranoia, I tuned everything out and concentrated on Dane's scent.

I opened myself up to him in a way I hadn't allowed since Quivira.

It wasn't hard. It was a relief.

Dane was surrounded by a group of men, but as soon as his eyes met mine, a flood of feelings came over me, making my blood sing. I wasn't sure whether the feelings were mine or his, or one and the same, which made it all the more alluring. I was all tangled up in him, and we weren't even touching.

He excused himself, and although I knew they were probably watching us, we only had eyes for each other.

He looked down at my feet. "I see some of Quivira stuck with you."

"But not with you," I said, studying him, looking for the slightest trace of the boy I'd met at the junkyard. He seemed perfectly at ease here among these horrible people. It made me wonder how much influence Coronado had over Dane.

"This will do, even though I'd have preferred the other dress." He looked me up and down. "But something's missing."

"Oh, I know," I said. "It's the entire back of this dress. Thanks for that."

"The pleasure is mine. Truly." He smiled, that sexy dimple

peeking out. "I know what it is," he said, pulling a black silk ribbon from his pocket.

"It can't be." I reached for it, the ribbon coiling around our wrists. To outsiders, it would look like nothing more than the wind picking up the strands, but I knew better.

I felt the darkness rise inside of me. It felt too good not to be dangerous, but I didn't step away.

"Love will always bring us back together," he said as he stepped behind me, fastening the ribbon around my throat. I hadn't worn it this way since Quivira. I thought it would feel suffocating and wrong, but it felt like it was the only thing holding me together.

"Are you ready?" he asked, caressing the length of the ribbon, his knuckles skimming my spine, sending a surge of electricity through me.

"Yes." I exhaled a shaky breath.

"Then it's time for you to work your dark magic," he whispered in my ear.

I tried to play it off, but the goose bumps exploding across my skin gave me away. In that moment, I hated myself. I hated my blood, for answering to his touch so easily.

"Where would you like to start?"

I scanned the crowd, making a concerted effort to look into every set of eyes that dared to meet my gaze. I remember how that felt, having Katia stare at me that way. I could've sworn she was looking straight into my soul.

I gravitated toward a man and a woman standing near a bronze sculpture of a sea nymph. Easy prey.

"Please, introduce us," I said to Dane, in a low, controlled voice as we approached a stout, red-faced Englishman, accompanied by a glamorous woman with lush red hair, her long delicate throat dripping in emeralds. She was relatively new; I could smell it in her blood. He must've paid a hefty price to have her made.

"Grant and Ellen Davenport, may I present Katia Ashlyn Larkin."

"We've met," I said, remembering his profile in the notebook.

"Yes." His eyes raked over me. "How marvelous it is to see you again. We were beginning to wonder whether you would show."

"But now here you are," the woman said, a futile attempt at sincerity. "And look at the two of you. Blood bound. A love for the ages."

"You don't know the half of it," I murmured into my glass as I took a healthy sip.

"Where have you been hiding all this time?" the woman asked.

"The Americas. But your husband already knew that." I looked at him pointedly, remembering from Coronado's notes how he'd made his fortune in the Indian Wars.

"Honestly, who can remember? The years slip by so fast," Mr. Davenport sputtered. "The 1700s were a complete wash for me."

They both laughed like being on a hundred-year bender was charming.

"Yes." I took in a deep breath, feeling a dark tickle in the back of my throat. But it wasn't a tickle, it was a whisper. Coaxing it forward, I narrowed in on him like a crow pecking at a carcass. "The tribes you slaughtered on the shores of the Narragansett . . . do you hear them screaming in your dreams? Is that why you don't like fire? Do you smell their charred flesh in the flames?"

"H-how do you know about that?"

Mrs. Davenport pulled her hair seductively over one shoulder, kicking up the distinct scent of bloodlust.

"And you," I said, turning my attention on her. "Does your husband know you've slept with half the men at this gathering? Including my immortal mate." I took a step toward her, watching her eyes dart from Dane to her husband and back again, the slightest quiver in her bottom lip. Leaning forward, I whispered in her ear, "You're lucky I'm in a forgiving mood. Now run away before I do something I may regret."

Her husband grabbed her by the wrist, pulling her across the lawn.

"Well done." Dane tried to suppress a smile. "That was a bit risky, guessing the details of the slaughter, but I'm quite certain Coronado wasn't on the list of Mrs. Davenport's conquests in that little book I gave you. How did you know?"

"Black magic, of course," I teased. But how *did* I know? It was so subtle, a tiny hint of recognition, a tug in her direction. Maybe it was just female intuition, but I could smell it on her. As for the details of the slaughter, that came in clear as a bell, a distant whisper etching that horrible scene into my consciousness.

"A little harsh calling her out like that in front of her husband, though."

"Believe me. I went easy on them. He knows. He's only pretending to be appalled."

"Wow. Okay. That definitely wasn't on the list," he said as he dragged his hand through his hair. "You're not jealous that she slept with Coronado, are you?" He grinned down at me.

"Please." I forced a throaty laugh. "Look at her over there, trembling, telling the others how I got into her head. She's doing half of my work for me," I said as I watched her from across the lawn. But maybe I was a little jealous. After all, Coronado was now a part of Dane. I still wasn't exactly sure what that entailed, but I didn't want her thinking she had any claim to him.

A couple strolled over. Curiosity overruling caution. I didn't need an introduction. It was Brent and Julie Bridges. I'd know them anywhere from those late-night infomercials Beth liked to watch. *Bridges to Youth.* They were the official face for the Arcanum's exclusive serum. No wonder those actors never seemed to age; they were probably ingesting immortal blood like water. They also peddled a more affordable line for the masses, which did absolutely nothing.

Dane said, "May I present—"

"I know exactly who they are," I replied, taking them in, letting my eyes linger, but they didn't seem afraid, only more intrigued.

"It's amazing what you've done for Coronado. We were getting a little tired of his face, too," Brent said with a laugh. Julie nudged him, and he cleared his throat. "A vessel. Imagine getting a new body. A new identity. Julie and I would do anything for the opportunity. No price is too high."

"Even your soul?" I asked. "Because that's what the Dark Spirit would demand."

"Souls?" he asked with a crooked smile. "You won't find many of those here. Most of us gave those up long ago."

"I suppose it would be difficult having to constantly reinvent yourself."

"On the contrary." He grabbed a canapé off a passing tray and popped it in his mouth. "The key to immortality is change. If you can embrace change, find a partner to weather the gales and fair seas alike with you, then immortality can be a gift. But if you let yourself grow stagnant, holding on to the old ways, soon you will move through decades like a ghost. Until you become one."

He was a charmer, to be sure. That might work with his clients, but even without Coronado's little black book, I could see right through him.

"How do you manage it?" I asked. "Living in the public eye?"

"The digital age has presented its own set of challenges for us," Mr. Bridges said, "but it's easier than you think. A few carefully orchestrated deaths and births"—he waved his hand around—"but this latest incarnation has us all breathless. We'll be getting in line for that as soon as you get the kinks worked out."

"Kinks?" I asked.

"Oh, I mean no offense," he added, quickly brushing it off, but I knew there was something to it.

"Honestly, a good makeup artist in your service can do wonders." Mrs. Bridges winked at me.

She was probably in her late thirties when she was made immortal. Slightest hint of a West Texas twang. If I concentrated, I could still smell the gunpowder and campfire embedded deep within her pores. Despite her carefully assembled appearance and designer clothes, that first life still clung to her, like dried blood beneath her fingernails. There was a sadness about her, a softness that only comes with loss. I wonder what led her on this path.

But her husband was something else all together. Coronado noted that Brent had won his immortality in a bet with a traveling alchemist in the 1800s. But what Coronado didn't know was that Mr. Bridges cheated in that game, then pulled a pistol from his sleeve, killing every player at that table for the chance at immortality. Once a swindler, always a swindler. Could he be the one supplying Spencer with names, resources?

"You're a card player, Mr. Bridges?" I asked.

"From time to time."

I noticed the twitch in his fingers.

"Have an ace up your sleeve?" I narrowed in on him. "I have a feeling you may have coined that phrase—what was it? Late May . . . 1855? Dodge City?"

He let out a chuckle, but the slight tremor in his hand as he lifted the glass of sparkling water to his lips gave him away. "I think it's time for a real drink. Anyone else?" he asked as he chased after a waiter. "Bourbon, neat."

"Excuse us," Julie said as she went after him.

"You certainly hit a nerve," Dane said as we watched her trying to soothe him.

"It's not him," I said.

"How do you know?" Dane asked.

"He may be a cheat, a swindler, but he's not the one supplying Spencer with names . . . resources. He has enough demons to contend with."

"Duly noted, but again, I'm pretty sure that information wasn't in Coronado's book."

"It's called improvising," I replied. But it was more than that. I knew it and I think he knew it, too. Something was happening to me—maybe it was only the power of suggestion, pretending to be Katia—but whatever it was, I felt completely attuned to my intuition. It was far from unpleasant. It felt good to let loose for a change. Maybe this was the darkness the alchemist spoke of. Maybe it'd been with me all this time and I'd just never allowed myself tap into it before. But I couldn't help thinking that maybe the darkness, however dangerous, would help me find Rhys.

"Never thought I'd see the day . . . the two of you together again." A man with perfectly groomed dark hair and beard to match approached. "But maybe this new version is more palatable for you." I didn't need to recall Coronado's notes to know his secrets. Devon Jaeger carried his sins right out in the open. Dime-sized blood diamonds in each ear. I could smell his greed, his dark proclivities seeping from his pores. He'd been trying to modernize the Arcanum for years—his latest obsession, chemical weaponry—but Coronado was his biggest opponent, or Dane was. "Such a noble deed, doing this service for us in exchange for Coronado's release from the council."

I felt the tendons in Dane's arm tense. When Timmons spoke of Dane's precarious position with the council, I wondered whether Mr. Jaeger was the one behind the threats. But if Mr. Jaeger was the one supplying my brother and Spencer with resources, I assume he would've killed Dane by now. Or maybe he had something else in mind for him . . . something far worse.

I raised my chin to meet his penetrating gaze. "Aside from being a rapist and pillager, I didn't realize you were a relationship expert, too."

"You don't remember me, do you?" His face lit up with mischief.

I looked to Dane, but he seemed just as surprised.

As he leaned in, it took everything I had to stand there and not recoil from him.

"Cat got your tongue," he whispered as he tugged on the end of the ribbon, slipping it out of the bow. "And such a lovely tongue, as I remember."

As he walked away, I tried to keep my cool, but it felt as if I couldn't swallow, couldn't breathe. Why didn't Coronado warn me? Did he not know?

"It's okay, *mi amor*," Dane said as he stepped in to retie the ribbon. "You did well. It's been a very long time."

Mi amor. The phrase slipped under my skin. I remembered

Coronado calling me that before he left the sacred circle in Quivira.

The wind found me, the salt air whipping my hair around my face like agitated snakes, and I heard the whisper. *Coronado knew.*

"You're surprisingly adept at this," Dane said. "I'm not sure if I should be impressed or afraid."

"Be afraid," I replied as I advanced on him, grabbing him by the lapels. "Because if you ever lie to me again . . . try to fool me . . . put me in harm's way, I will let my brother murder the world in order to destroy you."

"Ashlyn," he whispered, his eyes welling up with concern. "It's me . . . Dane."

I looked up and I felt him, every bit of him, his hurt, his confusion. It was him. I don't know why I did that.

Letting go, I backed away, across the lawn, toward the sound of the sea. Anything to drown out the phantom whisper in my ear. I couldn't believe I'd said that to him. It's like I wanted to hurt him. Is that how I really felt or did I get caught up in the moment? Was this the path to darkness that the alchemist spoke of?

Dane followed me, gripping my hand just before I was about to back over the edge of the cliff. Looking down, I felt dizzy watching the surf pound against the rocky crags, at least a hundred feet below.

"Maybe this wasn't the best idea," he said as he looked back at the crowd. "You can leave right now. I'll have my personal guards take you anywhere you want to—"

"No." I pulled my hand away, steadying myself. "I know what they'll do to you if I leave. I know they'll retire you, whatever that means."

"You know about that?" he whispered.

"Why didn't you tell me?"

"I wanted you to come *for* me, not because you felt sorry for me," he said as he looked down at the ground, at the torturous space between us.

I could feel the pain pouring off him and all I wanted to do in that moment was hold his face in my hands, tell him that I never gave up on him. On us. But for now, I needed to keep this all business, until I knew what I was doing . . . until I was sure.

"That's not why I came," I said, swallowing my feelings. "I came for my brother. That's all."

"Of course," he replied.

"I can do this." I squared my shoulders. "The cava went straight to my head is all. I just need a few minutes alone."

"Are you sure?"

I nodded.

He started to leave and then paused. "For the record, if I ever betrayed your trust again, you wouldn't have to lead Rhys to my door—I would look for him myself, and beg for a swift death."

As he walked away from me, I stood on the edge of the cliff, staring down at the roiling sea, blinking back tears.

At first, I thought he kept it from me to save his own skin. But the more time I spent with him, the more I came to understand that he didn't tell me that he'd been threatened because he didn't want me to feel manipulated. When he said his life was meaningless without me, I believed him. Because deep down, beneath all the bravado, I felt the same way.

Dumping the rest of the cava from my glass, I watched it soak into the terra-cotta soil, turning it bloodred.

17

"YOU OKAY, DARLIN'?" Mrs. Bridges sidled next to me.

"A lovers' spat . . . nothing more."

"It must be strange coming back here, after all this time. I always thought Coronado was a scoundrel, with that voracious appetite of his, but now I see the ladies were just a way to pass the time, ease his pain until you came back to him. And here you are. Giving him a run for his money. You go, girl."

"We have a complicated history."

"And he's a complicated man. I gotta tell you, we were all a little concerned when he came back. We weren't sure if he'd ever recover."

"How was he different?" I asked. "I mean, I should know if I want to work out the kinks."

She looked around to make sure no one was listening in. "Violent outbursts, talking to himself. I heard he cried himself to sleep every night."

I thought about Dane telling me there was a transition period, but clearly, he'd glossed over the details. I couldn't imagine how hard that must've been, especially having to come to terms with all of this in the public eye. I only had Katia inside of me for a few moments and I'd never felt so insane. There was no one helping him—no one to confide in. He had to negotiate this all on his own.

Except for Lucinda.

I scanned the perimeter of the party, seeking her out. She wasn't hard to find. Wherever Dane was, she was, orbiting him like a dark moon. I didn't know what her role was in all of this, but I intended to find out.

Mrs. Bridges was nice enough to try to introduce me around. I mingled with whoever dared to engage, but kept it light. I'd probably done enough damage for one evening.

As I watched Dane working the party, shaking hands, I wondered how long we'd be able to keep this up. I'd eventually run out of dirt to dazzle them with, and then what? Dane and I stole glances at each other, but he gave me my space. I hated hurting him like that, but it was necessary until I had a better grip over my emotions.

Looking around for a distraction, I noticed a man in a crisp linen suit and pink bow tie, dabbing at his forehead with a silk pocket square. He'd been dancing around me all evening. Max Pinter—the architect. I recognized him from his photo. Other than his affinity for male ballet dancers, Coronado gave me little else to go on.

I homed in on him, trying to breathe him in, but it felt as if there were a wall between us. Beyond the awful amber perfume and the acrid scent of his sweat . . . there was something else, something clouding my intuition. He was hiding something.

I circled him, and when he could no longer stand the anticipation, he turned to greet me, a strained smile plastered over his ashen face.

And there was a flicker of recognition. I remembered seeing him as we left the alchemist's shop. A moment of panic set in. Did Rennert tell him that I was an imposter? I forced myself to breathe. Play it cool. "We meet again."

"About that . . . I was only . . . he told me it would work . . . that it would protect me . . ." He fingered the small amulet hanging from a chain around his wrist. I took in a deep breath. Horehound and mandrake. An old brew believed to ward off hostile magic.

Pinter raised his voice as he gripped on to me. "I didn't want to do it."

"Do what?"

"They made me," he yelled.

Lucinda signaled for the guards.

"Who?" I asked. "What did they make you do?"

As the Arcanum guards closed in, he dug his nails into my wrist. "I know who *you* are. I know who *he* is. You're both in danger," he managed to get out before the Arcanum grabbed him, hauling him back. "Look at the plans. The plans!" he cried as I watched his heels digging a path in the soil.

Dane rushed over to me, inspecting my wrists. "Are you okay?"

"I'm fine," I assured him, trying to catch my breath.

Dane looked furious. "Have him thrown off the grounds at once," he yelled to the guards. "And sober up, man!"

As I looked around at the council members gathering, I saw the mix of fear, doubt, and horror on their faces.

"Give us a moment," he announced to the crowd.

Reluctantly, they stepped away to gossip elsewhere.

"I'm sorry you had to see that," Dane said soothingly. "Max is a gifted architect, but when Rhys's blood killed his partner, Terrance, last month, he started to slip. I had no idea he was this far gone."

"I saw him today in Barcelona."

"Where?"

I thought of telling him about the strange encounter at the apothecary, but decided to keep it to myself for now.

"I'm not sure, but he said he knew who I was. Who you were. That we were in danger. And something about plans. 'Look at the plans.'"

He shook his head. "He's clearly lost his mind."

"He wasn't drunk. He wasn't crazy. He was scared. I could feel it. We need to talk to him. If he knows the truth about us, maybe he knows something about Rhys, too."

He let out a heavy sigh. "I really think he's just gone over the edge, but if it will make you happy, I'll ask my personal guards to find him . . . bring him back."

"Thank you," I said.

He nodded, then turned to speak to one of the guards.

"All taken care of," he said as he returned to me.

As I looked around the gathering, the immortals hovering in small groups, I murmured, "They think I did this. That I made him lose it like that."

"Let them," Dane said. "The only thing separating us from a life of torment is their absolute fear of and fascination with you. Remember that. And whatever they would do to Rhys pales in comparison to what they'd do to us."

18

"BLOOD DRIVE AND cocktails in the main ballroom," Lucinda called out with a box full of needles in hand.

The crowd let out an unexpected cheer.

"Am I missing something?" I asked as Dane offered his arm to escort me into the main house. "Since when is a blood drive cause for celebration?"

"This is Arcanum business," he said as he led me inside. "The blood drive is mandatory. Twice a year, each member offers six pints of blood. The council invests the money. It's turned into a lucrative source of income for all of us."

"So, the council is basically a blood mob for immortals?" I said.

"They do a lot more than that. Whatever problem a member has, whether it's business or personal, it's brought to the table to be solved."

"*Solved*. Is that what they called ordering the death of my entire bloodline?"

Lucinda glared at me as we passed. "I hope she's not the one taking the blood."

"You'd be surprised. She has the lightest touch I've ever seen."

"What's her deal anyway?"

Dane leaned in. "She kind of came with the house. She's been here since the 1500s. Coronado arranged for her immortality when he came back from the Americas. I know she's a little sharp around the edges, but she can be trusted. She helped me with the notebook. She's the only one who knows about me . . . my shared arrangement with Coronado. They were very close."

"Wait, do you think she and Coronado . . . ?"

Dane cringed a little.

"Oh God. That explains a lot. I heard he had quite a reputation with the ladies. And I quote, 'a voracious appetite.'"

I watched a blush creep over his collar. "Yeah. I've learned a lot from Coronado's memories. Some things I will never be able to unsee," he said with a sheepish grin.

As we approached the main hall, one of the Arcanum guards hurried past with an armful of tubing and blood bags.

He turned his head away as if he were afraid to even gaze upon me. Clearly, my reputation has preceded me. "Good thing I'm not afraid of blood."

Dane tightened his grip on my arm. "We can't participate," he said through his teeth as he smiled at a passing guest.

"Why?"

"Your blood has properties we don't want anyone to know about. Much too dangerous."

"How would they know?"

"Everyone will want a taste."

"What?" I stopped walking. "Why?"

He tenderly arranged my hair around my shoulders. "Immortals like to . . . well, let's just say it can get pretty freaky in there."

"Okay. Gross," I said under my breath as we continued walking. "But won't we draw suspicion if we don't show up?"

"No one would dare interfere with lovers who've just been reunited after hundreds of years," he said with a sly smile.

"What did you have in mind?"

Abruptly, he pinned me against the door to his study. I felt a rush of dark energy pulse through my bloodstream.

Pulling my hair back from my throat, he whispered in my ear, "Pretend you want me."

I laced my hands through his, and the euphoria that came over me was far from pretend. The closeness of his body made me short of breath.

A few people saw us, but I think that was the whole point.

Reaching behind me, he opened the door to his study and then swooped me up in his arms. I giggled into his neck as we stepped inside the darkened room, turning our backs on the world.

19

"THANKS FOR PLAYING along," Dane said as he set me down.

I turned away from him, positioning myself directly in front of the fire, hoping the heat would mask the flush of my skin.

"Drink?" he asked as he pulled the stopper off a crystal decanter, flooding the room with vanilla and spices.

"Better not. The cava kind of snuck up on me," I answered, still trying to get ahold of myself. "But don't let me stop you."

"I don't drink," he said as he replaced the stopper. "It's imperative that I stay in control."

"Is this about Coronado?" I finally worked up the courage to ask. "How do you manage it . . . with his soul inside of you?"

"It was especially tough in the beginning. There were times when I thought I'd go mad. Learning how to control it was a delicate negotiation, to say the least."

"But how does it work?" I asked.

I could tell by the way he avoided making eye contact with

me that he wasn't completely comfortable talking about it, but he consented. "I'm the dominant, but I let him take over when I need him, with running the business, interacting with the council, certain things I need to know. It's gotten easier. One day, it will be as simple as breathing," he said as he took a seat on a chair in front of the fireplace. "He's not as bad as you think."

"That's funny," I said as I perused the books and knickknacks placed artfully around the room. "I remember seeing him kill various members of my family. He wanted to kill me."

"He wouldn't have killed you," Dane leaned forward. "I know that now. He would've kept you for himself, and I couldn't bear that, either. Loving you is by far my biggest weakness," he said as he crouched in front of the fire, adjusting one of the logs to let in more air, and I couldn't help thinking about him doing the same thing in Quivira. A year had passed, and he still had the same effect on me. I was still waiting for the air to come.

"The council wants to get rid of you," I said. "And I feel fairly certain that as soon as I fulfilled my role, they would get rid of me, too. What would that even mean for an immortal?"

His jaw clenched. "We can be imprisoned. Immurement. I'll spare you the details, but I can't imagine anything worse . . . an eternity of hunger, thirst, and loneliness."

The way he said it, the hollow sound of his voice, sent a chill over me.

"There's something that's been bothering me," I said as I crossed behind him, watching the muscles in his back as he stoked the fire. "Why didn't you come for me sooner?"

He glanced back at me, as if he were surprised by my question.

"All that time, you were in control, you knew where I was. You knew how much pain I was in."

"You told me to stay away."

"And you do everything you're told?"

I watched his shoulders collapse. "I wanted to give you time. I didn't want you to feel like you were being manipulated, by my words, or your blood. I wanted you to be free to choose. The worst part of this past year was living with the guilt over what I'd done. What I put you through. But the main reason I stayed away was because I didn't want you to see me that way."

"What way?" I asked.

He stood to face me, a confession perched on his lips, but instead Dane leaned down and kissed me.

I wanted to pull away, but everything in my body screamed at me to give in. And when he parted my lips, every fear, every worry, every doubt seemed to dissolve like sugar on my tongue. In this moment, the ache to feel connected to him was stronger than my will. He kissed me with such a powerful need, a year of yearning, jealousy and hate, unspooling around us.

I felt the single button on the back of my dress snap off, my shoulders roll forward to slip out of the lace sleeves, his mouth on my collarbone. Arching my neck, I glimpsed the portrait of Katia, lit by the flames of the fire, our untethered passion, when reason set in. This was how I lost my head—this was how everything went so wrong to begin with. I couldn't afford to lose control. I couldn't let this happen until I was certain of who he was . . . who *I* was when I was with him.

It took everything I had to pull away. Slipping my arms back in the sleeves, I turned to leave, when I bumped into a suit of armor, sending the helmet rolling across the room like a medieval bowling ball.

"I'd be happy to escort you back to your room if you'd like."

"No." I held up my hand, trying to catch my breath. "Nope . . . I'm all good," I said as I listened at the door, making sure it was all clear. "For the record," I said as I unlocked the door, "I think you've gotten better at that."

"Or maybe you've just gotten worse." He grinned.

I stumbled out of his study, right into Lucinda.

"Well . . ." She looked me over, disapproval seeping from her pores. "Be off with you before you cause even more trouble."

I ran up the stairs, being careful to hold the top of my dress up.

Beth, I thought as I reached the top. I can't believe I forgot about her.

Sneaking down the hallway, across the breezeway, up the winding stairs, I pushed past the guards, ignoring their knowing stares, and burst into her room.

She was still in bed.

I sank down next to her, feeling the cool night air on my feverish skin. There was a strong astringent odor in her room, and underneath that, I could've sworn I smelled Rhys on her lips, but then I spotted his McNally Jackson bookstore T-shirt, tucked under her arm like a teddy bear.

"Rhys," she said as she gazed up at me.

"No, it's me . . . Ash."

"Oh my stars," Beth murmured as she focused in on me. "Did you get in a fight?"

"No . . . no." I tried to smooth down my hair. "Just . . . never mind about me. How are you feeling?" I squeezed her hand.

"I'm still so tired. But Lucinda's been looking after me."

"Really?"

"She gave me some medicine."

"What kind of medicine?"

"Yarrow."

I felt her forehead. If she had a fever, it was gone now. At least Lucinda knew her herbs.

"She told me a story, too."

"What kind of story?"

"A scary story . . . about her brother," she said with a deep yawn. "Something about true love . . . finally being free . . ." She began to drift off.

"Beth?"

"I'm sorry. Can we talk tomorrow? I can hardly keep my eyes open."

"Then don't." I smoothed my thumb over her brow, the way my mother did for me when I was sick. "You must need the rest. We can catch up in the morning."

I left her and skulked past the guards, down the stone steps to the first long corridor. This entire place was crawling with shadows, secrets. I trailed my fingertips along the stone, wishing the walls could talk. There must've been countless nights filled with music and laughter. Great love stories. Battles won and lost. As I skimmed my fingers over a door on the left-hand side, a whisper, a faint tickle in my ear, dared me to go inside.

I pushed open the door to find an austere room—an iron bed, dressing table, chair, and a bare window. The way the moonlight spilled in gave everything an ethereal glow. At first glance, it seemed simple, but there were hints of unexpected luxury and romanticism everywhere you turned—a pressed flower, a book of poems, rosary beads, a sable throw hidden beneath the worn cotton coverlet. There were candles everywhere, wax dripping decadently over the sides. I opened a drawer to find delicate lacy undergarments. On the dressing table, Chanel red lipstick. Loose powder with a feather puff. An ornately carved silver brush. The distinct smell of rose water and freesia. This was Lucinda's room. It felt strange seeing this side of her. A softer side. Tucked into a Bible was an old etching with Coronado's image, but he was much younger, then. I couldn't imagine how hard that must've been for her, watching Coronado come back a completely different person. But if she accepted Dane, helped him get through his transition with Coronado, she couldn't be that bad. At least that's what I kept telling myself.

Just as I was getting ready to leave, I heard footsteps coming up the stairs. I knew that scent, the assured click of the stilettos. Panicking, I closed the door and crawled under the bed.

Lucinda stepped inside and began pacing wildly, ranting in Catalan.

I caught a word here and there, but most of it was lost on me.

And then she dropped to her knees beside the bed, the edge of her skirt draped over my hand. I heard her thumbing through pages of a book. The rattling of beads. *"Perdoneu, Pare, perquè he pecat."*

Forgive me, Father, for I have sinned.

She was praying.

Something about sin. Light and dark . . . love and loss.

A knock on the door startled her, and she dropped her beads.

As she reached down to grab them, she yanked out a strand of my hair in the process.

Lucinda opened the door to the same guard who had cowered from me as we were heading to the ballroom.

"He's retiring for the evening," he reported. "Do you want company?" He reached out to touch her, but she slapped his hand away.

"Not now." Lucinda followed him out. As soon as she was gone, I let out a huge gust of air, but I didn't dare move a muscle until I was certain I heard their footsteps on the stairs. That was entirely too close.

When I could no longer hear anything other than my own heavy breathing, I bolted from her room, ran down the hall and across the breezeway, to the safety of my own room, locking the door behind me. But something was different. Someone had been inside. There was a note dangling from the crystal knob of the armoire.

This should get you through the next few days until I can take you shopping.

I flung open the doors to find a whole new wardrobe. Not just gowns, but sensible things like jeans and shirts and blazers. I cracked a smile when I saw the wedding dress hanging in the very back, but I didn't rip it from the hanger. Though I would've preferred to have my own things, I appreciated the effort to match my minimalist style.

As I took in the rest of the room, I saw that the bed had been turned down, a new fire had been lit, the cava had been replaced with sparkling water. There was a silver tray brimming with fresh bread, figs, pomegranates, nuts, cheese, and honey. My stomach growled at the sight of it. I didn't realize how starving I was. Loading up a piece of bread, I crammed it in my mouth and went into the bathroom to text Timmons. As I unearthed the phone from its creamy grave, I caught my refection in the mirror. My hair was a mess, no big shocker there, but my dress was ripped—there was blood smeared on my back and arms. I peeled off the dress and ran my hand over the marks that had already healed.

When I kissed him, it felt like this beautiful thing, but Beth was right. It really did look like I'd been in a brawl. Pretty symbolic.

Unwrapping the phone from the shower cap, I turned it on. Timmons's number was the only one programmed in.

I texted—Met other immortals on council. Pretty sure they think I'm Katia. But one man, architect named Max Pinter, seemed to know who I was & who Dane was. Said we're in danger and something about plan. "Look at the plans." He got kicked off estate. Dane pretty shaken up about it, said he's going to find him so we can talk. Can you look into alchemist in Barcelona named Rennert? Also, a woman here named Lucinda apparently "came with the house." She's gorgeous, creepy as fuck & she hates me. Good times. Tomorrow's a big meeting about Rhys & Spencer. Till then—Ash

It felt good to sign my own name.

I heard a noise in the hall and quickly rewrapped the phone, submerging it in the jar of cream.

There were footsteps heading my way. I knew they belonged to Dane. It wasn't just his scent. It was the rhythm of his breath moving in and out of his lungs. I reached out to him, trying to sense his emotions, but he was guarding them for some reason. He paused in front of my door, and I held my breath.

"We need to talk." Lucinda chased after him. "Look at what she's doing to you—you're exhausted."

"If you don't like what you see, you don't have to watch. You're welcome to leave at any time."

Lucinda stormed off.

As he went to his room, I walked the perimeter, following his footsteps, dragging my hands along the walls until I reached the door that separated our rooms.

Maybe it was only my imagination, but I swore I could feel him standing there, that if I whispered his name, he'd whisper mine back.

20

I AWOKE TO quiet.

No fire engines, people screaming, cars honking, kids playing in the street, or dogs barking.

But it wasn't silent at all.

There were donkeys braying in the distance, the ebb and flow of the sea, the wind moving through the trees, making the branches shiver, and the distant sounds of crows taking flight. In a way it was noisier than the city. All of my senses seemed amplified here. Alive.

I drew a bath. As I stepped into the steamy water, I heard the faint crush of seashells from below. Peeking over the windowsill, I saw a group of immortals gathering.

"She says she's Katia, but something doesn't feel right."

"You met her over five hundred years ago."

"Which she didn't recall."

"People change."

"People don't change. Not people like her. There's something about this whole situation that doesn't sit right with me. I don't like it. After all this time she agrees to show up just as we're being systematically murdered. For all we know, *she* could be the one behind this. Think about it: Neither one of them was there for the blood drive. And before that little tryst in his study, she was cold as ice."

"They've been at war for centuries. Do you think she'd really forgive him, forgive any of us for ordering the murder of her ancestors?"

"But what of Max Pinter? What was all that about?"

"She must've been digging around in his head and he panicked. What was he babbling on about?"

"I know he's been doing a lot of work for the Arcanum lately."

"I don't see how anything she did had any mystical qualities. For all we know Coronado could've been supplying her with the information. He's always been a slippery bastard."

"We're keeping an eye on the situation. But for now, we need her."

"If she fails to deliver the immortal killer, we'll have no choice but to get rid of both of them."

I heard the door to my room opening.

"Do you mind?" I yelled over my shoulder and then clamped my hand over my mouth.

As the men looked up, I ducked down into the tub as quickly as I could, sloshing water over the sides.

"Relax, Miss Larkin," Lucinda chastised me.

The men below must've heard me, because when I peeked back over the sill, they were gone.

As soon as I heard the door close, I grabbed a towel and rushed into the room to find a breakfast tray full of pastries with fresh preserves and a complete outfit laid out on the bed with a note.

Meeting: main ballroom 11:00 a.m.

There was a black pencil skirt, a cropped cream-colored silk blouse, paired with some strappy heels.

"No thanks," I said as I threw on a pair of black skinny jeans, a soft gray T-shirt, and the least fussy shoes I could find—a pair of jeweled sandals.

Grabbing a piece of toast, I headed to Beth's room.

I pushed past the guards, only to find the door locked.

"Beth." I knocked. "Open up."

"I can't," she called back, but she sounded weird, like maybe there was a gag in her mouth.

"You better open this door," I said to the guards.

They ignored me.

"What's going on?" Lucinda said as she came up the stairs.

"Open this door. *Now.*"

She glared at me as she unlocked it.

"And don't give me those eyebrows."

As the heavy door swung open, I was prepared to find Beth gagged and weeping, but she was lounging in bed, in silk pajamas, her mouth stuffed with pastries. There were fancy packages strewn all over the place with new clothes, shoes, a computer, the whole series of *Murder, She Wrote*, but Beth had abandoned everything for a book. She could hardly tear her eyes away from it long enough to give me a casual wave.

I turned on Lucinda. "Why was her door locked?"

"For her own safety. She was found downstairs in the main hall in the middle of the night, weeping."

"In the same spot?"

Lucinda seemed flustered. "If someone had seen her—"

"I'll deal with it," I said as I turned my back on her.

Lucinda fluffed Beth's pillow and smiled down at her warmly. "You have no idea how happy I am to see you looking so well."

Somehow, nice Lucinda was even more unsettling than mean Lucinda.

As soon as she left, I moved a box of chocolates aside so I could sit next to Beth. "What's going on?" I asked.

"Oh, I'm at the part where Daniel walks in on Clara . . . with the music teacher. I mean, how could she? Doesn't she know how much he loves her?" she asked as she dipped a churro into a pot of thick chocolate and took a huge bite.

"No." I took the book away. "I mean why were you downstairs?"

"I dreamed about Rhys. I heard something. I felt something. Maybe it was a ghost." She shrugged, reaching for the book.

I looked at the spine. *"Shadow of the Wind,"* I whispered. "Where did you get this?"

"Dane brought it to me early this morning."

"Did you know this is one Rhys's favorite books?"

"Really? Oh, now I love it even more." She grabbed it and hugged it.

"Did Dane bring all of this?" I asked as I looked around.

She nodded. "He likes to spoil me. In Quivira, he was always sneaking me lemon cakes from the Mendoza lodge. But *this*," she said as she looked down at the tray of pastries. "This is even better." She dipped another churro into the chocolate, forcing me to eat it.

It was delicious, but extremely sweet.

"Maybe you should lay off the sugar a little. How about a piece of fruit? A pear? A fig?"

"No way." She pulled the tray onto her lap, like she would cut me if I tried to take it away. "I'm happy as a lobster."

I didn't bother correcting her. "What did you talk about . . . with Dane?" I asked, wondering if he'd mentioned our kiss.

"We talked about Rhys." She grinned, her chipped tooth peeking out. "How nice it's going to be when we're all together again." She grabbed a rolled-up piece of paper from the other side of the bed. "Look, he brought this."

I unrolled it to find blueprints.

"He's building a whole wing just for Rhys, so I can visit him any time I want. With safety glass and everything."

"Safety glass?"

"Because of his blood, silly."

It felt like I'd been punched in the gut. I hadn't thought of that. If Rhys didn't want to be with us, if he wanted to harm us, he'd have to be contained. What kind of life would he have? He'd never be able to be with Beth . . . in that way. He'd never have children. Dane was building this to make sure Rhys couldn't hurt anyone ever again. As much as the plans gutted me, I couldn't help but feel a surge of tenderness for Dane. The way he cared for Beth. The way he wanted to care for my brother. For me.

"There's a meeting about Rhys. After that we're going to make a plan of our own. I think we can do this. We're going to find him. We're going to help him, no matter what."

The clock in Beth's room struck eleven.

"I have to go," I said as I sprung to my feet. "But I'll come check on you later this afternoon."

"Take your time," Beth called after me as she went back to her book.

I caught myself practically skipping down the stairs. I told myself it was just so I could find out more information, but I knew it had something to do with that kiss.

If I pressed my fingers against my lips, I could still feel him there. And God help me, but I couldn't wait to feel that again.

21

AS SOON AS I entered the bustling room, a hush fell over the crowd, but the dark whisper persisted.

My friend from last night, Mrs. Bridges, patted the seat next to her. As much as I wanted to sink into the background, be a fly on the wall, Katia would never give away her power that easily. They may not think much of Coronado, but they were in his home, and he was my immortal mate. We needed to show strength, now more than ever.

Dane was standing off to the side, speaking with a few of his guards, but when our eyes met, it was as if he'd understood everything. I remembered feeling like that in Quivira. We didn't need words to communicate, because we were perfectly in sync. I forgot how seductive that could be.

He signaled one of the guards, and a chair was brought over, set down in *front* of the front row. That said everything.

"Now, to the matter at hand," Dane said as he pushed a button to lower the screen and dim the lights.

Before he started, he gave me the strangest look—it was as if he were apologizing for something in advance. But the moment he closed his eyes, I felt his nerves evaporate.

When his eyes opened, they focused in on me with an intensity that registered in every molecule of my body, an undeniable attraction, but the anguish, the guilt had vanished.

As he went over the details of the recent casualties, I couldn't help noticing that there was something hypnotic about the way he took the stage, commanding the attention of the room. I'd heard of people taking on roles when they had to perform, but this was something else entirely.

"We've identified three culprits who we believe are responsible for these killings," he said as a photo of Spencer and Teresa popped up on the screen. They were walking on either side of a person slumped in a wheelchair, wearing a baseball cap. It was Rhys. It was the same photo that Dane showed me in Barcelona, but this was the full image.

I wanted to scream out, *Why is my brother in a fucking wheelchair?* but I bit my tongue.

The three of them were together. This was undeniable proof. But maybe Rhys wasn't doing it by choice. Maybe he was hurt or they were drugging him.

"Where was this photo taken?" a spindly woman with a thick German accent inquired.

"It came from a port surveillance camera, Valencia, four days ago. We're assuming the boy in the wheelchair is the source of the blood," Dane said.

"Who are they?" a man from the back called out.

"We're still working on putting names to faces, but these individuals don't appear to have a digital footprint, which leads us to believe they were raised off the grid."

"Maybe someone from that cult of hers in Kansas," someone murmured. I recognized his voice as one of the men outside my window this morning.

"I'd watch your tongue," Dane said as he paced the stage. "Katia believes there's someone paying for these murders, someone who has inside knowledge of the council. Someone in this room."

A rush of electricity swept through the crowd.

I clenched my hands into fists. Why would he say that? Get them all riled up like that.

"Funny they would target Rhinebeck and Perry and Wells," Mr. Davenport said. "Your biggest critics on the council."

"What are you implying?"

"Merely stating a fact."

"Have there been any demands?" Mr. Bridges asked. "They must want something."

"Only the betrayer knows what they want. But Katia is narrowing her scope as we speak. She said last night was very . . . *enlightening.*"

The crowd became restless. I was afraid to turn around, afraid they could see my fear.

"How do we know it's not her behind this?" Mr. Jaeger said, stoking the flames. "Or if she's even Katia?"

The hush that fell over the room was deafening. Even the familiar whisper held its tongue.

Dane lowered his chin, staring daggers into Mr. Jaeger, and it gave me the chills. "Is this all because she didn't remember your thirty-second encounter in the rose garden hundreds of years ago? Or maybe *you're* the one behind this. Maybe you want to use this boy's blood as a weapon, and now you're getting rid of anyone who would stand in your way on the council. You've always had a fondness for war."

Mr. Jaeger stood, knocking his chair to the ground, but the others took hold of him.

A satisfied grin tugged at the corner of Dane's mouth. A cruel streak I didn't recognize. "If any of you have even a sliver of doubt, it will be quelled tonight. After dinner, a special package will arrive—the sheets from the *Queen Isabel*, from the cabin of our murderer. One whiff and Katia will be able to tell us everything about this immortal killer."

When Dane met my eyes again, something ripped inside of me. A schism in the atmosphere. I knew that face. It was the same smug expression he had when he left the sacred circle in Quivira, with my mother's ashes still clinging to the bottoms of his boots.

The man standing before me wasn't Dane—this was Coronado. It was so subtle. The way he held his head a little higher, his shoulders squared, like he was wearing armor all the time. While Dane moved with youth, Coronado moved like a man of the world.

I sank back in my chair, watching him, trying not to think about everything he'd done to my family, what he'd done to Dane . . . to me.

"And when we catch this boy, this killer of immortals"—Coronado looked right at me, as if he were taunting me—"we're going to find the deepest, darkest vault and send him straight to hell."

I bolted from my seat. "Dane. Enough."

He closed his eyes for a moment, and when he opened them, I felt Dane, the boy I fell in love with, come flooding back to me, full of shame, regret, and sorrow. "Until tonight," he said softly as he cleared his throat.

As the immortals filed out of the room, I stood there, unable to move, unable to blink, trying to come to terms with what I just witnessed.

When the room was finally clear, Dane reached out to touch me and I flinched.

"Why didn't you tell me? Warn me?"

"I told you I have to rely on Coronado to get through certain things."

"But I didn't think you'd disappear . . . become an entirely different person."

"Like it or not," he said, his eyes welling up, "he's a part of me now."

"But how could he tell them that? You know I can't *do* any of that."

"Do what?"

"Find the immortal killer by smelling dirty sheets."

"Is that what he said?" he whispered, staring off toward the screen.

"Yes! He promised them all a brilliant demonstration after dinner tonight."

Dane took a deep gulp of water, his brow knotting up in confusion.

"Wait. You really don't know what he said? You're kidding, right?"

"Things can get murky in the transition." He rocked back on his heels as if he felt woozy. "Look, I don't know why he said that, but it's not the worst idea. It's a great diversion and we're so close—"

"If I hadn't said your name, pulled you back, what would've happened?"

"I would've come back eventually. But the important thing is that you *did* pull me back, just as I was able to pull you back from Katia in Quivira."

"But I don't *have* any powers, or have you forgotten that, too?"

"Pretend, like you did last night. You were amazing. Remember that we're weaving a narrative—"

"For them to 'retire' us?"

"A narrative where Rhys doesn't have to die."

I knew Dane had come back to me, body and soul, but I couldn't stop picturing what that was like, seeing Coronado's cruelty shine through Dane's eyes . . . move through Dane's lips. And I couldn't shake the feeling that Coronado loved seeing me squirm.

"Ashlyn," he whispered as he reached out for me.

"No." I backed away. "I need space right now. I don't know what Coronado's playing at, but I don't like it. A friend told me to listen to my instincts . . . and my instincts are telling me something isn't right here," I said as I turned to leave.

"We were able to track the gold," Dane called after me. "I didn't get a chance to tell you before the meeting."

I stopped. "What do you mean?"

"Twenty gold bars were auctioned off at Sotheby's last month."

"So . . . they were probably mine."

"No. Yours bear a Q with a line through it."

"How do you—"

"Because I've bought every bar," he said softly. "The ingots I'm referring to were your mother's work. And they had Spencer's fingerprints all over them."

The memory of Spencer slitting my throat and stealing the case full of cash and ingots flashed in my mind.

"We're tracing the money as we speak," he said. "It was funneled into an overseas account. Spencer wouldn't know how to do that. He's getting help from someone. Someone who's probably here with us right now." Dane glanced toward the door. "Within forty-eight hours, we should be able to trace the account to an address. And hopefully, to Rhys. We just need a little more time."

"But how can I trust you? When half of you belongs to someone I hate? When he can take you over so easily?"

Dane's knees seemed to buckle as he grabbed the edge of a chair to steady himself.

"Are you okay?" I asked.

"Of course he's okay," Lucinda snapped as she entered the room, helping him to a seat. "But he needs his rest." She grabbed my arm, escorting me to the door. "You're only making things worse. I don't know what you're doing to him, but when they find out you're nothing but a cheap imitation, who do you think they'll punish first? Or do you even care?"

"What?" I asked in shock.

"A little advice . . ." She pushed me into the hall. "A seasoned immortal would never expose their feelings in that way, so recklessly. They're on to you. You should run."

She shut the door, locking it behind her.

Lucinda knew who I was.

She knew the truth.

22

I RAN OUTSIDE to the formal garden . . . to the hedge maze.
I needed air, but more than that, I needed to find a place away
from prying eyes, away from his scent. I ran until I hit the center
of the maze, a large rectangle, with high hedge walls all around
me. As I sank to the ground, I wept—for myself, for Dane, for
my brother, for everything that had gone so wrong.

Seeing him like that—being possessed by Coronado—was
almost too much to bear, but Dane had taken care of me, stood
by me, when I was possessed by Katia. He brought me back
every single time. He didn't judge me; he didn't love me any less.
Why couldn't I do the same for him?

A murder of crows rose from the hedge maze, all at once,
circling overhead like a warning.

As I got to my feet, I heard footsteps approaching through the
maze. A single heart pounding. It wasn't Dane. It wasn't Lucinda.

Wiping away my tears, I backed against the far hedge,

preparing myself for anything. Whoever this was, they'd followed me here. This wasn't a chance encounter. The scent of wood smoke, juniper, and wild rose hit my senses.

"There you are," Julie Bridges said as she peeked her head around the corner.

I let out a sigh of relief, my shoulders dropping at least a few inches.

"Am I interrupting?"

"Not at all. I was just heading back in," I said as I tried to walk past her, but she blocked my path.

"Can I have a moment? Woman to woman."

But Julie wasn't here to chitchat. She wanted something. I could smell it on her.

"It's about Coronado," she said. "The council would like to offer you a remedy. A gift, if you will."

"What kind of gift?" I asked.

"Immurement." She swallowed hard. "Retirement. We can take care of that for you . . . if he's a problem."

"What kind of problem?" I asked as I took a step toward her, feeling a strange dark heat move through my limbs.

"Maybe he's getting in your way." She stepped back. "Maybe it would be easier for you to concentrate if he were . . . out of the picture."

"Are you offering to get rid of him as a gift?" I said as I pinned her against the hedge. "Or are you threatening to take him away from me as punishment?" I asked, feeling the darkness rise to the surface.

"That's entirely up to you," she said with a shuddering breath as she watched the black silk ribbon uncoil from my wrist and slither up her arm, to ease around her neck.

"All you have to do is find the immortal killer, and all of this will end," she blurted. "You and Coronado will be free."

"Squeeze," I whispered, summoning the black strand to tighten around her throat. "If any harm comes to Coronado . . . they will answer to me. To the Dark Spirit. Are we clear?"

Her eyes bulged, her face was so red I thought it might explode, but she managed to nod.

"There now," I said, and the black strand released, slithering down her arm to coil once again around my wrist.

She fell to the ground, clutching her throat, gasping for air.

"And the next time the council has a message, they may come to me directly. No need to send a sacrificial lamb. Or there will indeed be sacrifices."

23

WITH A FIXED gaze, I walked back to my room. I wasn't even sure what happened back there . . . if it was the ribbon or just my imagination, but I was afraid of what I might do if I saw one of the council members right now, afraid of what I was capable of. I wondered if this was the darkness taking over. If this was the beginning of the end.

As I opened the door to my room, I found Lucinda inside, packing my belongings.

"We have no use for these. Dane wants you to keep them as a token of his appreciation."

"I'm not leaving." I took the clothes out of her hands. "Not until I find my brother."

She clutched the amulet around her neck and gave me the strangest look, like she was desperately trying not to cry. "You need to leave."

"Look." I let out an irritated sigh. "I get it, you don't like me.

You had some kind of relationship with Coronado. But things are different now. We're blood bound—"

She took in a hissing inhalation of breath as if my words had offended her in some way. "You have no idea what you're talking about. What that even means. Where were you when he needed you? You weren't here to put him back together again. You have no idea what he's had to endure. The agony he's gone through to try to gain control. To reach you. You didn't listen to him cry himself to sleep every night, worrying over you."

"Well, I'm here now."

"And what about tonight? The immortals have gathered to watch a brilliant display of dark magic."

"All I have to do is smell a sheet and act creepy, which isn't much of a stretch for me these days."

"A child's response. This isn't one of your games. The council suspects something's not right with you, and if I had it my way, I'd let them tear you to pieces. But I know Dane, and he will protect you with every bone in his body. To his peril."

"What do you want from me?"

"When this goes wrong, and believe me, it will, you need to confess. Tell the council that you tricked Coronado into believing you were Katia. If you do that, I will help you escape. I will deliver your brother. You have my word."

Part of me wondered whether she was doing this to protect Dane, or whether this was just a sick way to get Coronado all to herself again. But it didn't matter. The last thing I wanted to do was put Dane in harm's way.

152

"If I'm backed into a corner, I'll take the fall," I said. "You have my word."

"I'll make the preparations," she said solemnly as she turned and left the room.

I locked the door. Not that it would make any difference.

I was scared—for me, for Dane, for all of us, but I kept going back to Beth's vision—the four of us together under a snowy sky, but it wasn't cold. I believed in her and I needed to believe in him. That he could control this. That he could bring Rhys home.

I started to head downstairs when I looked at how I was dressed. Sure, I was comfortable, but I remembered what Lucinda said about behaving like a seasoned immortal. If I was going to do this, I was going to do it right.

Opening the armoire, I thumbed through the dresses. "What would Katia wear?" My fingers stopped on a tight oxblood dress that zipped all the way up the back. It was perfect.

I brushed out my hair—which was no small feat—and pulled it back from my face, twisting it into a sleek French twist, securing it with a jeweled comb.

I used the makeup. Not just my usual stroke of mascara and some lip balm. I *really* used the makeup. After three tries, I managed a halfway-decent smoky eye and paired it with a nude lip. Coiling the black silk ribbon around my wrist, I slipped my feet into a pair of deadly heels.

I made my way downstairs and stood in front of the dining room, taking in one last steeling breath.

This was it. The moment of truth. The moment of lies.

As I entered the dining room, Dane stood and the rest of the immortals followed suit.

I felt their stares as I passed, like icy liquid fingers on my skin, but I kept my eyes trained on Dane, who sat at the far end of a long banquet table.

As I approached, Dane pulled my chair out for me, but I surprised him by stepping in close, pressing my lips against his for a kiss. The warmth traveled all the way down to the tips of my toes.

"Sorry I'm late," I announced. "I didn't get much sleep last night."

A low chuckle erupted throughout the room.

Dane smiled at me. The sexy smile I knew belonged only to him. And we all sat down.

Let the games begin.

24

"IF YOU'RE TOO tired, we can postpone tonight's demonstration until—"

"No. I'm ready," I said as the staff cleared remnants of grilled octopus from the table. I leaned back in my chair and crossed my legs seductively.

Dane signaled and one of his guards brought over a sealed plastic bag that contained a crumpled sheet. He placed it on the table in front of me.

I couldn't bear doing this in the full light of the chandeliers. "I need candlelight and quiet."

Dane nodded and the waitstaff brought in two additional candelabras and dimmed the lights.

I looked around the room . . . at each and every face, bathed in shadow and light. Some were frightened; especially Julie Bridges, she could hardly look my way. Most seemed wary, but Mr. Jaeger sat there, arms crossed over his chest, a smug look on his face. He didn't think I could pull this off . . . that I had it in me. But I would do *anything* to keep Dane safe, and to find Rhys. If putting on some kind of immortal magic freak show helped our cause, that's exactly what I was going to do.

Grabbing a carving knife off the sideboard, I walked around the entire table, slow and deliberate, remembering what it was like to have Katia inside of me. The assuredness, the venom racing through my veins. When I reached my place, I stepped up to the table and stabbed the bag dramatically. I took my time sawing through the thick plastic. I wanted each notch in the serrated blade to register on the backs of their necks.

When I sensed I'd built up enough tension, I pulled the sheet free, pressing it to my face, breathing it in. I closed my eyes, letting my mind wander to the sacred circle in Quivira when Katia summoned the Dark Spirit. I began whispering in Caddo. At first, it was pure gibberish, but soon the words began to take shape into something more—as if they were coming from a well, deep inside of me. I didn't know if it was the dim lighting, the energy in the room, or pure performance, but I began to feel something move through me, caressing every molecule in my body. There was a strange tingling in my chest that grew until I felt my rib cage expanding. As the words began to flow, a voice whispered back, cooing in my ear. Slipping off my heels, I crawled onto the table, knocking over glassware and silverware in my wake. Grabbing the candelabras, I tipped them, letting the deep red wax drip onto the olive wood table. Digging my fingers into the scalding wax, I released whatever was inside of me, feeling it move through my hands. The sensations were muddy at first, but as soon as I locked in on him, my brother came in crystal clear. "I'm in a dark room. I can't move. There's a slow drip, a hissing sound, and then I feel it: a stinging warmth exploding in my veins. There are dull thuds coming from above. The creaking of doors. Laughter and a voice I recognize—a voice so much like—"

"Ashlyn."

I come back to my body to find Dane standing before me, a look of panic in his eyes.

I looked around the room to see everyone craning their necks, staring down at the table in dark fascination.

Following their gaze, I saw there was something spelled out in the wax, a number 16028-593, along with the word *underfoot*.

"What does it mean?" someone whispered.

All I could do was stare down at my trembling hands, the thick coat of red wax encrusting my fingertips, cutting me off from my senses.

"She needs time to process," Dane said as he picked me up in his arms.

"That's it?" Mr. Jaeger said. "I've seen better performances at the pantomime. And you called her Ashlyn. We all heard it."

"Ashlyn is Katia's middle name," Dane said, all the muscles in his body on edge.

"Have I rattled you, Mr. Coronado?" A vicious smile curled across his lips. "How interesting."

I could feel Dane's anger reach a boiling point. I looked to

Lucinda to help, but she just stood there, urging me with her dark eyes to speak up, confess, but I wasn't ready to give up so easily.

As Dane set me down to confront Mr. Jaeger, I kissed him. It was long and languorous, full of so much passion I thought the entire room might burst into flames. Without a word, Dane took my hand, leading me out of the room.

We didn't look back, but I could feel their eyes on me—every doubt, every fear, every jealous thought, a searing lash across my skin.

25

WHEN WE REACHED our corridor, he walked right past my door, opening his own.

I had to admit I was curious to see his surroundings, and I didn't want to be alone right now.

I stepped inside; the rich wood-paneled walls were lit by candlelight. The windows were wide open with a small fire crackling in the fireplace. It was like stepping back in time.

He started to take off his tie.

"You know that kiss down there was only for show, right?"

"Can't blame a man for dreaming." He smiled up at me through his dark lashes. "You were brilliant, though. I wasn't even sure if you'd show up. Thank you for that, for rescuing me," he said as he got a washcloth from the bathroom. "If I had to listen to one more story about the bubonic plague, I was going to stab myself with my dessert spoon."

"You should know . . . the sheet . . . what I felt . . . what I wrote in the wax . . . that was real."

With a furrowed brow, Dane reached out to take my hands in the hot towel, easing the wax from each of my fingertips. "Ashlyn, the sheet was brand-new."

"That can't be," I whispered as I pulled my hands back. "I smelled my brother. I felt him. He was there."

"The power of suggestion can be very convincing—"

"No, it's more than that. They're drugging him. They're taking his blood against his will. I'm sure of it."

"Okay." He nodded. "The numbers, the words—do they mean anything to you? Anything at all?"

"No." I swallowed hard. "Maybe I'm just being crazy—"

"No. I'm going to alert my team. See if they can come up with any leads."

"Thank you."

"For what?"

"For believing me."

He reached out to touch my face but stopped himself. I wished he hadn't.

As he retrieved his phone from his bedside table to send a text, I browsed the gemstones lined up on a wood inlaid console table on the far wall, but these weren't the crude varieties he kept back at Quivira. They were giant gleaming cut stones— emeralds, rubies, tanzanite, and some I'd never seen before.

"That one would look stunning on you," he said as he put his phone away and picked up a gray stone with a deep sparkle, as if it held a tiny universe inside. "It's Musgravite, one of the rarest gems in the world," he said as he kissed it, placing it in the palm of my hand.

"My mother told me to never accept jewelry from strangers."

"Sound advice, but I'm hardly a stranger."

As I returned the stone to the table, I thought about how little Dane and I really knew about each other. I didn't know his favorite color or who taught him how to read, but I knew other things like the taste of his lips, the shape of his jaw when he was proud, and the exact light that made his eyes look more blue than brown. And above all, I knew his scent, better than I knew my own.

Dane reached behind me to adjust the stone so it was in the exact same position as before.

"I see you're still a neat freak," I said.

"I take care of the things that matter to me."

"Am I a thing to be taken care of?" I asked.

"No." He looked at me intently. "*You* are everything." He skimmed his fingers along my waist and I longed to lean in to his touch, to feel the full weight of his hand on the small of my back.

When he pulled away, I let out a measured breath. "Mr. Jaeger's clearly going to be a problem. Do you think he's the one behind the killings?"

"It's hard to say. But in my experience, he's always been openly contentious. This is different. It takes a special type of personality to kill using poison. There's hidden emotion and a duplicity that will be hard to detect. No, whoever's behind this has unprecedented access, but it's someone operating from the shadows."

"I don't trust any of them," I said.

"I'm afraid the feeling is mutual." He let out a sigh.

"Why didn't you tell me that Lucinda knew the truth about me?"

"She asked me not to. She wanted to see how convincing you could be."

"You know she came to me earlier, pleading for your safety. If things went badly tonight, she asked me to confess, tell them I was an imposter, that I deceived you. In exchange, she said she'd help me escape. She'd help me find my brother."

Dane seemed shocked by this. So much so that he had to sit down on the sofa in front of the fireplace.

"Lucinda, she's been acting strange lately."

"Let me guess . . . since my arrival?"

"I suppose so," he replied. "She cut me with a letter opener today. Said it was an accident, but she's not the clumsy type. I don't remember saying anything to anger her."

"You tend to have that effect on people."

"Maybe." He tried to smile, but it didn't take. "I thought she understood, but—"

"But what?"

"It's probably nothing. She's used to being the only lady of the house, is all."

"You could ask her to leave."

"This is her home. More than it is mine. It's hard to imagine this place without her," he said as he looked around.

Following his gaze, I perused the room, running my fingertips along a sword mounted on the wall, medals, trophies, all belonging to Francisco Vásquez de Coronado. I wondered why Dane kept it all—just to maintain the illusion? There were so many things I wanted to know—things I needed to know if we were going to take this any further. And what did we have to lose? At any moment the council could burst in here and do God only knows what to us. I didn't know how much time we had left. And I couldn't waste another second.

"Drink?" I asked as I turned away from him, trying to gather the nerve to go through with this.

"Please, feel free," he said as he stoked the fire.

Removing the stopper from one of the decanters, I took in a deep whiff of something resembling airplane fuel. I knew that smell . . . from the bonfire at Quivira. "Corn rye?"

"What can I say? I'm sentimental," he said as he settled back on the sofa.

I poured two glasses.

"I'd love to join you, but as I said, I can't afford to dull my senses. Especially not in your presence."

"You might want the drink after I tell you my request," I said as I took a seat next to him.

"This sounds ominous." He took the glass.

"If I'm to have any future with you, it has to be built on more

163

than desire, more than our blood. I want to know you, completely. And in order to do that, I need to see you. All of you. And you were right, like it or not, Coronado is a part of you now. I need to know exactly what I'm dealing with. How much is you. How much is him. I need to be sure I can *feel* the difference. I want to speak to him. Alone."

"Sick of me already?" He tried to make a joke out of it, but I could tell he was uncomfortable by the way his breath hitched in his throat.

"What are you afraid of?" I asked.

"I don't even know where to start, but I've never given up complete control to Coronado."

"But today at the meeting, I saw what happened—"

"When I let him take the lead. I'm still there. I'm watching, listening. It's like an out-of-body experience. What you're asking me to do is dangerous, on so many levels."

"I can bring you back. Just like you did for me in Quivira. You experienced it today at the meeting."

"That was different."

"You said love will always bring us back together. If you truly believe that, you'll do this for me."

"Ashlyn—"

"I need you to trust me. Like I trusted you."

He drank his rye in one shot.

I did the same, nestling my glass in his, curling my legs up on the couch in anticipation.

"If he does anything—"

164

"I can handle myself, but if he does anything . . . *untoward*, I'll bring you back so you can kick his ass. Deal?"

He looked at me with such anguish as if he were memorizing every detail of my face. "I love you," he said, before closing his eyes.

As I was trying to catch my breath, trying to figure out how to respond, I watched an ease roll through his muscles, melting away the tension in his brow. And when he opened his eyes—I knew. There was a dark glint that didn't belong there. A smile curled on his lips, but it wasn't Dane's smile.

"At last, a moment alone." He sighed as he eased his hand along the back of the couch, touching the jeweled comb holding up my hair. "May I?" he asked as he slipped it out, running his fingers through my hair, arranging the unruly waves around my shoulders.

"That's better." He slid his hand onto my bare knee.

"I have questions," I said as I removed it.

"Of course you do." He got up, crossing over to the bar. "I would expect nothing less from such a clever girl," he said as he dug an old bottle of port from the back of the cabinet. "Graham's Vintage Port, 1963. I received a case of this in lieu of a debt." He opened the bottle and took a deep whiff. "Clearly, one of the best decisions I made during the sixties."

I studied every facet of him, the way he moved, the way he spoke, trying to discern every detail.

"Dane doesn't drink."

"I am not Dane." He looked over his shoulder, giving me a

slight wink. "This is a rare opportunity and I plan to make the most of it."

"Rare, in what way?"

"To be untethered." He slipped the tie from his neck and took off his jacket, rolling up his sleeves. "Between us, he's a bit of a bore. Frankly, I don't know what you see in him. Or maybe it's *me* that you see in him. That must be it or you wouldn't have arranged this little rendezvous," he said as he prowled toward me.

"Only because you're a part of him. If being with Dane means being with you, I need to understand exactly what that means."

"I've mentored him, coached him," he said as he settled next to me with his drink. "I don't live in darkness, if that's what you're asking. I see what he wants me to see but, unfortunately, I'm not privy to everything, nor is he privy to all of my thoughts. I'm here when he needs me. Nothing more."

"And you're content with that?"

"Strangely enough, yes. It helps that we have a common interest." Coronado's eyes skimmed all the way from my ankles to my collarbone. "Dane's will is stronger than mine. His love for you keeps him in control. I could never overpower him even if I wanted to. And believe me, I've wanted to." He coiled the end of the black silk from my wrist around his finger.

"And you should know, I'm not Katia."

"No. You most certainly are not." He took a sip of his drink, the scent of deep plums, ripe cherries, and fragrant flowers clinging to his lips. "Physically, there's little difference. You even have the same tiny freckle below your right—"

"Yeah, I got it," I said as I crossed my hands over my chest. "I've seen the portrait."

Coronado smiled. "But there's a hardness about you . . . a darkness that not even Katia possessed. Even the veins in your arms seem aggressive," he said as he traced the bulging blue vein from the inside of my elbow to my wrist.

I pulled my arm away.

"You're really the perfect marriage."

"That's wrong on so many levels."

"And yet here you are, involved with Dane and his great-great-great-great-great-great-great-great-great-great-grandfather. I ask you, what's worse?"

"Not by choice."

"We'll see." He set his glass down. "By night's end, you may forget about him entirely." He reached out, stroking his fingers along my cheek. There was no hesitation in him, no fear.

And the darkness in me let him do it. There was a part of me that wanted to know what his touch would feel like. It was still Dane's hand, but there was an emptiness there. A hollow space, begging to be filled. With Dane, every touch, every glance, every word was loaded with our past, present, and future. Being with Coronado was simple. It was Dane's body without any expectation, nothing more than our base desires, flesh upon flesh. It would've been so easy to slip into the abyss. For a few fleeting moments, to forget who we were, who we were supposed to be.

He leaned in, brushing his lips against mine, and I found myself easing into him. He smiled at the way my body seemed to react, his eyes lighting up with mischief. But as he went in for the kill, I bit down hard on his lower lip, forcing him to look me in the eyes.

"Dane," I whispered.

A look of pain and rage passed over him, as if I'd betrayed him in some way. He closed his eyes and when he opened them, I felt Dane come back to me, flooding me with emotions—a hypnotic cocktail of blood and guilt and sorrow. Suddenly, I was desperate to feel connected to him, like I couldn't get close enough to him if I tried.

I kissed him, really kissed him. Breathing in time, our limbs entwined. I craved him in a way I hadn't felt since we were together under Heartbreak Tree.

"Ashlyn, stop."

"Why?" I panted.

"I'm bleeding," he said as he dabbed his lip.

"I don't mind," I said as I went in for more.

"But you need to know." He held my shoulders. "It's my blood that's making you feel this way."

"I don't understand."

"When immortals share blood, well . . . it's a very intimate thing to do. But being blood bound intensifies everything."

As his lip healed, the desire quelled, but it didn't completely dissipate. It felt as if I were drunk with him, with the promise of his blood.

Dane tried to stand, but his knees seemed to buckle under him.

"Here, let me help you."

"I'm sorry," he said as he reluctantly let me lead him to his bed. "I didn't want you to see me this way."

"What way?"

"Weak," he said as he sank down on the edge of his bed.

"But this is all my fault," I said as I slipped off his shoes, forcing him to lie down.

"Did you get the answers you were looking for?"

"You really weren't there? You didn't see what happened?" I asked.

"No, but I'm guessing from the cut on my lip that he tried to kiss you."

"Something like that," I replied as I fixed his pillows, feeling a little guilty for letting it go that far. This confirmed that they could keep things from each other. I was glad. I didn't want Coronado knowing all the intimate details of my relationship with Dane. "You gave yourself over to him fully, just as I asked, and I was able to bring you back. That's all I needed to know," I said as I sat on the bed next to him, tracing my finger around the buttons of his shirt. "What was it like?"

"Darkness," he said with a shiver. "With each breath, I felt myself disappearing, until I could hardly remember the sound of your voice . . . your face."

I lay down next to him, in the crook of his arm, resting my head on his chest. I remembered what that was like, disappearing into Katia. How frightening that was. "I won't ask you to do that again."

"But I will, if it gives you peace." He looked down at me with tears in his eyes. "I'll do it again and again. As many times as you need."

This was the real Dane. Sacrificing everything for me. Again and again. I wanted him more than I ever had. It wasn't a rip-your-shirt-off kind of passion, but there was a sweet sadness about him. I wanted to fix him. I wanted to make him whole again.

"I had no idea about the blood, that it would feel like that every time. I'll never forget what that was like, feeling your blood course through mine under Heartbreak Tree. It felt like I was holding your heart in my hand."

"You were. You still are."

I leaned forward to kiss him, just as Lucinda barged in the room. She stood on the threshold in a sheer nightgown, her dark hair loose and wild, clutching something behind her back. "Pardon," she said as she quickly ducked out of the room, but the look on her face was undeniable. She wasn't just in love with Coronado, she'd fallen in love with Dane, too. And I was clearly in her way.

"I should go," I said as I started to untangle myself from him.

"Stay with me . . . for a little longer."

I looked up at him, at his weary, beautiful face. "I'm not sure if I can trust myself."

"Then don't," he whispered with a tempting smile.

There was nothing I wanted more than to be with him, in that way, in his fine bed, in his arms, in blood. But I couldn't give in to this. Not until I knew my brother was safe.

"Good night," I said, forcing myself to leave his bed.

As soon as I reached the safety of my room, I let out a heaving breath.

Pacing the floor, I tried to come to my senses. "I'm stronger than my blood. I'm stronger than my blood," I whispered to no one.

I removed the heavy iron key from the agate box. The metal quickly warmed to my touch. I stood in front of the door that separated our rooms. All I had to do was slip the key into the lock and he'd be mine. Or I'd be his. But I needed to think with my head and not my "heart."

I took a deliberate step away from the door. I thought not seeing him would be enough to quell my blood, but being this close and not being able to touch him was pure torture.

Climbing into bed, I nestled the key to my chest and cried myself to sleep.

Somehow I knew he was doing the exact same thing.

26

I AWOKE FROM a nightmare to the sound of the key rattling in the lock. I had a brief moment wondering if it was the immortals coming to get me, but I could tell by the smell of brioche, blood orange, and black tea that it was breakfast.

I pretended to be annoyed, but this was the first time in I don't even know how long that I wanted to get up. I wanted to see what the day would bring.

I wanted to see *him*.

Lucinda brought in a large shiny white box with a breakfast tray balanced on top.

"This is for you to wear this morning," she said as she slid the box onto the bed.

"Look." I grabbed a brioche from the tray. "I'm not some Barbie doll you can dress up and play with," I said as I opened the box. "Last night was a one—Ooh . . ." I ran my hand over the thick cream cloth of the breeches. The gold buttons on the black blazer with a prim white shirt and the most luxurious pair of tall black boots.

"This morning, you ride," Lucinda said as she started to make up the bed with me still in it.

"I haven't ridden a horse since I was a kid. And that was a pony at a birthday party," I said as she bullied me out of the bed.

"Good. Maybe you'll fall and break your neck, come to your senses, and leave this place," she said as she left the room.

I felt like I should say something to her after last night, but what could I possibly say? I didn't know what kind of arrangement she had with Coronado . . . what he promised her . . . but everything was different now. The sooner she faced it, the better. I knew why she wanted to get rid of me, but I wouldn't scare so easily.

Taking in a deep whiff of oiled leather, I thought, what do I have to lose? I can't die, and it beats sitting around watching Beth get diabetes.

Putting everything on, I checked myself out in the mirror. I might fall on my ass, but at least I'd look good doing it.

I grabbed a fresh green apple from the bowl at the foot of the staircase and headed toward the stable. I didn't need to ask for directions; the earthy scent of fresh-cut hay and saddle leather was enough to lead me.

I was surprised to find Dane there by himself, saddling up a couple of horses.

"I thought you'd have stable boys for that," I said.

"I like to do it myself." He glanced back before putting the bridle on the jet-black horse. "It's peaceful. Everything is simple here. It's just you and the horse. If you can make a horse trust you, you can't be that horrible of a person."

"You're good at making people trust you."

Instead of the usual snappy comeback, he paused, his face cast in shadows. "I deserved that," he said quietly as he continued tightening the straps.

I raised the apple to take a bite when the other horse snatched it right from my hand.

"Hey!" I laughed.

"This one clearly belongs to you," he said. "Her name is Ash."

"You named a *horse* after me?"

He put the bridle on her. "I needed someone to talk to." He smoothed his hand over her face. "She's beautiful and graceful. The color reminds me of you."

"Gray?"

"Not just gray. She's a dapple gray. When she runs, she looks like smoke."

Tentatively, I reached out to pet her, but she pulled back, violently shaking her head. Dane slipped his hand through mine, and we stroked the horse together.

"Be firm with her." His eyes flashed toward me. "Ash is a tricky one. You don't want to show her that you're afraid or she'll get the upper hand."

"And what's wrong with her having the upper hand? She's a lot more powerful."

"Because she won't respect you." He pulled his hand away, and a tiny revolt went off inside my body.

He led the horses out of the paddock. "Put your foot in the stirrup."

I started to put the wrong foot in when he corrected me. As I rose up to swing my leg around, he gave me a boost.

"Was that really necessary?"

"Probably not." He smiled. "You want to hug the horse with your legs," he said as he ran his hand up the length of my thigh. "The pressure will keep you in the saddle."

"Don't I need a helmet or something?"

"Afraid you might die?"

"I wish," I murmured under my breath, but I didn't mean it. Not today.

"Don't worry. We're going to take it nice and easy," he said as he checked the reins.

"Why? Because I'm a girl?" I asked. "What if I don't want it nice and easy?"

He looked up at me and grinned. "We can certainly accommodate." Dane slapped my horse on the hindquarters, and she took off out of the stables. It was terrifying at first, this beast moving beneath me, all muscle and fury, but after a few moments, I got the hang of it, more or less. I loosened my grip and tried to move with the animal. This was the closest to flying I'd ever felt.

Dane tore out of the stable and circled in front of us, slowing us down, leading us toward a well-worn path.

"Did you know the conquistadors brought the horses to America from Spain?" he said as we meandered through the orchards. "Andalusians, just like these. Before Coronado went into the plains, the natives had never seen a horse before."

"Do you see his memories, like I saw Katia's?"

"It's not the same as it was with you and Katia. I saw what that did to you." He seemed to shudder at the thought. "It was hard at first. Some of the memories were so terrible that I wanted to dig them out of my head with a pickax, but other things were nice. The prairie grass swaying in the wind. Katia laughing with the sun in her hair, butterflies dancing all around her. Most of the time, Coronado's presence is as thin as a whisper. Sometimes his influence is as simple as a food I crave that I've never tried before."

"Hence the octopus," I said.

"Hence the octopus." He grinned. "But sometimes it's a mutual sadness. When I look at the portrait in the study, or when I watch you walk away from me, his pain mirrors my own. That's something we share."

As we passed a tree, Dane plucked a piece of fruit from one of the branches. He pulled up the edge of his shirt to rub it clean, exposing his toned stomach. His gorgeous olive skin. I tried to look away, but it was too late. The smile spreading across his lips told me he knew everything. He sidled up next to me, kissing the fig before handing it over.

I took a bite; it was warm and ripe from the sun . . . from

his lips. "Delicious," I said as he led us past the fruit trees to a seemingly endless grove of silver-leafed trees.

"What are these?" I asked as I skimmed my hand along the delicate branches.

"Olive. This grove is more than a thousand years old."

"It's beautiful."

"We can learn a lot from these trees," he said as we wandered down the rows. "Look at the trunks. Some are graceful, elegant in their form, while others are gnarled and bent. But even when they are stretching out to the far corners of the earth, they remain connected, their roots tangled up in one another's. An unbreakable bond."

And I wondered if that's what Dane and I were like. If we'd always end up twisted together in one form or another.

"This tree should be our signet if we ever marry. Think about it: Mrs. Dane Mendoza Coronado," he said with a sly grin. "It has a nice ring to it."

"Do you ever let up?"

"Never when it comes to you."

He reached out for my hand. As good as it felt, I pulled away.

"I know what you're feeling," he said. "It's a mix of emotions, but I still can't tell what you're thinking. You look a million miles away."

"Our past," I said as I stared up at the slow-moving clouds. "It feels like a weight. My mother told me that when I fall in love, I'd carve out my heart and throw it into the deepest ocean.

That I'd be all in—blood and salt—but I don't want to live on the bottom of the ocean floor. I can't remember the last time I felt light."

He took in a sharp breath as if my words had cut right to the quick of him, of me, of everything we were under the Heartbreak Tree.

"Look, we don't have to talk about this," I said.

"I want to. I want you to be able to tell me anything. I know I hurt you, but I want to make it up to you. All I want is for you to trust me again."

I took in a deep breath. "It's more than that. More than us. You'll never understand what it means to kill your mother. I don't know if I'll ever be free of that guilt and how it's connected to you."

"I want to show you something," he said as he took off, his horse in a full canter. As we rode through the countryside, I tried not to get caught up in him, how masterfully he handled his horse, the way the wind caressed his hair, the way the light seemed to bend to his face. He was stunning and fascinating, and he was in love with me. But there was still something holding me back. I didn't know if it was pride or fear or just plain common sense, but I needed to make peace with this. The fracture between my head and my blood was tearing me apart.

When we reached a narrow lane leading to the ruins of a castle, we dismounted, letting the horses graze in what once must have been a courtyard, but was now overgrown with dark green clover.

"Why would anyone abandon a place like this?" I asked. "It's magical."

"The amount of money needed to restore an estate is considerable, but there's also the matter of it being cursed."

"Cursed?" I asked as I followed him inside the structure.

"There was a lord who lived here in the thirteenth century. He had a beautiful wife, Isabel. When the lord returned from a crusade, he heard rumors that his love had been unfaithful, and he called for her immurement."

"Immurement," I whispered. That's what the council had threatened me with. "That's Latin . . . right? What exactly does it mean?"

"I believe the translation is 'walling in.'"

"So, he locked her in a tower, like a fairy tale?"

"Not exactly. He cemented her in a small space in the wall. This wall," he said as he nodded toward the crumbling stones. "She cried out for days and days. More than a week had passed when he discovered the rumors were false; that she had indeed been true to him. He tore open the wall, but it was too late. She was already dead."

I put my hand to the remnants as if I could somehow feel her presence, but I felt nothing but cold stone.

"But night after night, he still heard her screaming," Dane said. "He was haunted by what he'd done. In an attempt to make amends he had these made." Dane leaned down, wiping years of dust away from a tile. It read EGO SUM QUI PECCAVI.

"'I am he who has sinned,'" he whispered. "Every single tile in this castle says the exact same thing. He wanted every step he took to remind him of what he'd done. What he'd lost."

"Why are you showing me this?" I asked, rubbing the chill from my arms as I stared at the long expanse of tile.

"I don't need tiles to be reminded of my sin." He took my hand placing it against his chest. "It's in my blood. With every beat of my heart, I'm reminded of the pain I've caused you. Can you ever forgive me?"

This was the first time he'd properly asked for my forgiveness. But in truth, the moment I decided to come to Spain, I knew I would give Dane a second chance. But I hadn't been doing that. How long was I going to punish him? I wondered if in some sick way this had become habit, my way of relating to him. And I didn't want to live in the past anymore. In regret. I saw what that did to Katia, how it haunted her, changed her. I didn't owe this to him—and certainly not to Coronado—but I owed this to myself. The freedom to choose with an open heart. This wasn't the same boy I fell in love with at Quivira. This was a man who'd accepted the consequences of his actions. And now it was time to accept mine.

As we stood on the threshold of this cursed palace, I kissed him.

The scent of sandalwood, mandarins, musk, and sea salt permeated the thin veil of space between us. With my hands in his hair, his lips everywhere, a flood of ravens rushed toward the open blue sky as the black silk ribbon danced all around us.

27

WE RODE BACK to Castell de Coronado to find the courtyard swarming with immortals and guards.

"Something's happened," Dane said as he peered ahead.

I followed his gaze to a body laid out on the ground, covered with a stark white sheet.

"Stay here—you don't need to see this," Dane said as he started to turn his horse.

"Is it Rhys?" My heart hammered as I spurred my horse into a full gallop, with Dane chasing after me.

Jumping off the horse, I pushed everyone aside, yanked off the sheet to find Max Pinter, black blood seeping from every orifice, his face frozen in a state of final agony.

"Where did they find him?" Dane came up behind me, bracing my shoulders.

"Right outside the gates."

"This was a message," I whispered to Dane. "Whoever's behind this didn't want him to speak to us."

"Step back," Lucinda said as she snapped on a pair of surgical gloves. "There's something in his hand."

Prying open his clenched fist, breaking a few fingers in the process, she pulled out a long strand of dark blond hair, holding it up to the sunlight for everyone to see. While everyone was gawking at it, trying to guess who it belonged to, she turned her attention on me, the slightest hint of glee in her eyes. A look that said, *Gotcha.*

The rosary beads. That must've been the same strand of hair that was coiled around her beads the night I was nearly caught in her room. She was trying to set me up for this. Could Lucinda be the one behind all this, pulling the strings? Or did she just see an opportunity to get rid of me?

"We'll have the results back in twenty-four hours," she said as she placed the strand in a clear plastic bag.

As Dane took my hand, leading me back inside the castle, Mr. Jaeger followed, spewing accusations.

"I don't need to wait for the results"—he pointed at me—"it's her. I know it."

Everyone began shouting over one another, when Dane yelled, "Quiet!" But I could tell it wasn't Dane anymore. It was Coronado, all the way from his piercing stare to the controlled way he moved his body. "I can assure you, Mr. Jaeger, this has nothing to do with Katia."

"If that's even her real name," he answered back. "For all we know you found some stray who looks like her, paid your alchemist to make her immortal, coached her."

"I'm warning you."

"What are you going to do, give her another fake sheet? Make her sniff it like a dog?"

Coronado pulled a sword from the wall, and sliced Mr. Jaeger's throat open.

No one screamed. No one moved. No one dared take a breath.

As Mr. Jaeger dropped to his knees, clutching his throat, gasping for air, Coronado stalked over to me, slipped the blood-slicked sword into the bow of the black silk ribbon that was holding my hair back, and pulled it free. "That's better."

He met my eyes, daring me to say Dane's name. As frightened as I was, I didn't want Dane to come back like this, holding a bloody sword, not knowing what happened. I told myself that I was only trying to protect him, but I knew there was more to it. This show of brute force was necessary to keep the council in check. More and more, I understood the dynamic between the two of them. And I felt awful for even thinking it, but there was a part of me that didn't really mind. Grabbing me by the back of my neck, Coronado kissed me in a way that made me feel alive and ashamed all at once. My will unspooled around us, like molten fire forming around his touch. And when he abruptly pulled away, the look on his face told me he knew my innermost fear—that on some level, we were one and the same.

But then I thought of the alchemist's words: *to dance with the darkness . . . to dance with the light . . . which one will you choose?*

I'm stronger than my blood.

"Dane," I whispered, a single tear streaming down my cheek.

I felt him come back to me in a surge of confusion and remorse. He looked down at his hands, dropping the sword in disgust.

As Mr. Jaeger's throat began to heal, Dane handed him his handkerchief, but that was as close to an apology as he would get.

As the crowd dissipated, carrying Mr. Jaeger with them, Dane and I were left alone.

"I know you probably didn't realize it was him," he said. "But when you kissed Coronado, I thought I might shatter into a million pieces."

"I'm sor—" I started to say before he stormed off. He couldn't even look me in the eyes. Coronado wanted Dane to feel that. I felt sick and depraved for hurting him that way. For letting it happen. On some level, wanting it to happen.

As I watched the maids mop up the blood, I thought of Timmons. The last thing I wanted to do was worry him, but this was getting out of control. I had to tell him what was going on . . . about Max Pinter. About Lucinda. Because it was only a matter of time before the council took matters into their own hands.

Rushing up the stairs, to my bathroom, I opened the jar of cream to find Timmons had already sent me a text. **Meet tomorrow—café 3 pm Urgent. Watch yourself. Lucinda can't be trusted.**

I'll be there, I texted back. **Can I have any more info? Were you able to get in touch with the alchemist?**

As I sat there waiting for a reply, I glanced in the mirror. There were tiny dots of blood spatter strewn across my face. I scrubbed it off with a washcloth. But I would never be clean. I could still smell Coronado on my skin . . .

Shaking off the guilt, I had to figure out how to get into town tomorrow without drawing attention. I needed to talk this out. Rhys was usually my voice of reason, but Beth would have to put down her book and churros long enough to hear me out, because all I could think about was being immured. Walled in with no one to hear me, nothing to do but replay my mistakes over and over again in my head. Go mad. Dane had told me every estate had an immurement chamber. I wondered whether there was one here. And what would happen to Beth and Rhys if Dane and I just disappeared? The thought made me sick to my stomach.

As I walked to Beth's room, across the breezeway, down Lucinda's corridor, every creak, every shadow made me feel like someone was going to jump out and take me.

I eyed the guards as I stepped into Beth's room. What if they were more loyal to the council than to Dane? What was to stop them from turning on us, too?

But my paranoia took a backseat when I saw Dane sitting on the bed, next to Beth, holding her hands.

"Is everything okay?" I asked.

Beth looked up at me with tears in her eyes. "They're keeping him underground."

Dane explained, "We followed your lead from last night and just got word that the same company who brokered the gold for Spencer rented medical equipment. A hospital bed, IV apparatus, hazmat suits."

"Underfoot," I whispered, thinking of the word I'd scrawled in the wax.

"You were right." He looked at me in anguish. "Rhys isn't doing this by choice."

"Where is this place? We need to go there. Now."

"We interviewed the men who worked the job, but they were blindfolded and then taken to the location. They remembered going down two flights of stairs to a windowless room with concrete walls. It was unusual, but not unheard of. Some of their wealthiest clients do this when they're setting up safe rooms."

"So they're using him. Keeping him prisoner," Beth said with a trembling breath.

"We're going to find him. It could be a matter of hours or a few days, but I'm going to make this right. I will protect you and Rhys and Beth . . . no matter what."

Beth hugged us both. It was heartbreaking thinking about what Rhys has had to endure over the past year, but I had to believe that Beth's vision would come to pass. And Dane was somehow the key to its happening. I believed in him. And for the first time since Quivira, I believed in us.

"You're needed downstairs," Lucinda said as she slipped soundlessly into the room, making me flinch.

I tried not to make it too obvious, but I had to talk to him about her. Warn him. "Dane, I have to—"

"Soon," he said as he kissed me on the cheek.

I stayed with Beth, listening to her talk about Rhys. She asked me what was wrong, but I couldn't bring myself to burden her with anything else.

Instead, I hugged her and we stayed like that until her body stopped trembling, until she'd fallen asleep in my arms.

I knew it was late by the clang of dishes being scrubbed in the kitchen, the midnight sky seeping through the heavy leaded-glass windows. I went to Dane's study, and when I raised my hand to knock, I heard voices.

I heard a struggle, followed by a grunt of pain.

I tried to open the door, but it was locked.

"One moment," Dane called out, followed by a shuffling of feet.

And when Lucinda answered the door, she pushed past me. "Leave this place and never return, or you will suffer the consequences."

I entered the room to find him bracing his wrist. "Are you okay?" I rushed over to him. "Is it broken?"

"I'm fine. It was probably an accident," he said as we watched it heal. "She's stronger than she looks."

"This isn't right."

"I'll deal with it. I promise. But I want to know how you're doing with all this?"

I was speechless that he was just going to brush this off.

I wanted to tell him my suspicions about Lucinda, but that's all they were at this point. I needed proof. Maybe Timmons would be able to provide that. After everything that'd happened, Dane still trusted her. She'd seen him through a difficult time, and it was going to take something undeniable to make him see her for what she really was.

"How's Beth?" he asked.

"She was pretty upset, but she's asleep now."

"That's good." He nodded, but he seemed distracted, like he was gearing up for something. "I'm sorry . . . about earlier. I don't know how things got so out of control. But I don't blame you for being curious about Coronado. He's a part of me and however you need to make peace with that, I'm okay with it."

I wasn't sure what my face was doing, but I was so embarrassed, I felt like my cheeks might burst into flames. "It won't happen again," I assured him, but even as I said it, I didn't know if I could keep that promise. "I need to go into town tomorrow. Do a little shopping."

"Of course," he said as he crossed over to me. "What time shall we go?"

"No. It's for undergarments." I glanced up at the portrait, thinking she could really use some, as well.

"Well, in that case, I insist," he said with a weak smile.

"Nice try, but this is a solo trip." I pulled my hair back into a low ponytail, securing it with the ribbon. "I won't be long. Just a few hours."

"With everything that's going on," he said as he settled on the sofa in front of the fire, "I don't think that's the best idea."

I knew he was right, but I needed to meet Timmons. If my gut was right and Lucinda was the one behind all this, Dane was in a lot more danger than I'd even imagined. It was time to protect him for a change. I hated being mean to him, but it was the only thing that would get him to back down.

"I don't think you understand. I'm not *asking* for permission."

He looked at me curiously.

"I can always call a taxi if it's too much of an inconvenience."

"No." He softened. "It's no trouble. A car is always available to you. But it's dangerous out there right now, especially with Max Pinter's death so close to home."

"I'm not susceptible to Rhys's blood. You know that. I'm in no danger."

"There are worse things than death for an immortal."

"Keeping me here *is* walling me in. I have to be free to come and go as I please. I have no desire to go back to compound living, like in Quivira."

"I don't want that for you, either, but what will I tell the others? They need to believe you're in as much danger as they are."

I shrugged my shoulders. "I'm full of black magic, remember?"

"You're right." He swallowed hard as he turned back toward the fire. "I'll take care of it."

I felt awful for putting him in this position, but it was necessary.

"Are you coming up soon?" I asked, running my hand over his shoulder.

"I wish." He glanced down at my hand. "I have a few more things to deal with and then I might take a ride. Clear my head."

I sensed a chill between us. Maybe I'd overplayed my hand, but I didn't want to clue him in until I was absolutely sure.

"Well, good night," I said.

He reached up, squeezing my hand. "You are the most important thing to me. I won't apologize for wanting to protect you." He kissed the palm of my hand and folded my fingers into a fist, just like he did before we walked the corn together to face Katia.

It made me feel as if he were preparing me for battle.

28

AFTER A RESTLESS night watching the door to my room, waiting for Lucinda to creep in and hack me into a million pieces, I got up with the sun. I'd hoped to sneak out before anyone woke up, but when I went to grab the phone from the jar of cream to see if I had a new message from Timmons, it wasn't there anymore. I tore through the bathroom hoping I'd just forgotten to put it back, but I knew I had. I also remembered the look Lucinda gave me as she was leaving Dane's study last night. I wondered if she went into my room and took it. Wouldn't put it past her. I thought about using a house phone, but like an idiot, I didn't write down the number.

Since I'd already blown my plan of an early getaway, I checked in on Beth, before heading downstairs.

The immortals were unusually quiet. I wondered whether the hair analysis had come back early, but I couldn't worry about that right now. The only good thing was that Lucinda was nowhere in sight. I couldn't stand to look at her traitorous face this morning.

Walking down the long seashell path, past the gates, I found a car waiting for me. There was a driver already inside. Dane's personal guard opened the back door for me.

"I can drive myself," I said.

The guard looked past me, toward the gates, giving a slight nod.

The hint of mandarins and sandalwood slipped over my senses, making my blood come alive. Dane.

"Did one of those vipers tell you I was leaving?"

"I wouldn't need anyone to tell me that," he replied. "I could feel you walking away from me. The ache in my chest."

Peering over my shoulder, I tried not to get caught up in him—how good he looked, strolling through the gates, in a button-down, his hands thrust casually into the pockets of his linen trousers.

I wanted to tell him my suspicions about Lucinda, but I didn't want to start tearing his world apart until I was absolutely certain.

"Is this really necessary?" I asked, nodding to the two Arcanum guards now in the front seat.

"I kept my promise. You're lucky I'm not sending you in a tank."

"But—"

"You can always call that taxi. They should be here in a few hours, three tops," he said as he ran his hand down my arm, giving me goose bumps.

"Has anyone ever told you that you play dirty?" I said.

"I don't know what you're talking about," he said as he maneuvered me to take a seat in the back. "I'm an angel. You won't even know they're there."

"Doubtful," I said as I glared at the back of their heads.

"Take her to Mersilla's," he said to the driver. "It's the finest lingerie shop in Barcelona. It's in the Barri Gòtic. Very discreet. Oh, and this is for you." He handed me an American Express black card.

"Thanks, but I can buy my own underwear," I said as I tried to hand it back.

"The pleasure's all mine." He held his hands in the air, refusing to take it back. "Truly."

I wasn't sure if I wanted to punch him in the mouth or kiss him. But that's how it always seemed to be with the two of us.

As soon as we pulled away, I noticed an identical car following. No doubt it was full of Arcanum guards.

He wasn't going to make this easy.

29

THE RIDE BACK to Barcelona was tense. The silence. The wondering what would happen. I never put the café's address in the phone or Timmons's full name, but whoever took it knew that I was meeting someone.

The lingerie shop couldn't be far from the café. I could always go inside and ditch them, crawl out of a window or something.

As we pulled up in front of the shop, I thanked them for the ride and tried to hop out, but of course they had the safety locks on.

Dane's guard slowly got out and opened the door for me.

I looked around to see if the other Arcanum car was close by, but I didn't see anything. Maybe I was being paranoid.

"This could take a while," I said as I glanced up at the shop, dreading going inside. "You know . . . women and their shopping. You might want to go get lunch or something . . ."

But he just stood there, stone-faced.

Letting out a deep sigh, I turned and trudged up the stairs.

As I entered the shop, the smell of synthetic rose hit me, giving me an instant headache. There was classical music, Vivaldi. The bras and panties were on blush-colored, silk-padded hangers, strung out around the store like dainty confections. I glanced at the price tag on one of the bras and nearly gasped out loud. Four hundred euros for a bra? Oh yeah. Dane was definitely paying for this.

A slim, well-kept woman in her fifties approached. She looked me up and down like she was trying to decide if I was going to steal anything. I must've passed inspection because she started going on and on about my breasts having the proper support and air and whatever else she was spewing. I pretended to listen, but I really just needed an exit plan.

I thought about trying to do the whole small-talk thing, but I didn't have the time or the patience to go through the pretense.

"Here." I handed her Dane's credit card. "I need all the basics."

She glanced down at the name on the card and her eyes lit up. "I thought you looked familiar."

Familiar? I'd never seen this woman in my life. Had she been to Coronado's house and seen the portrait? Did she know about him and his "voracious appetite"? I wouldn't be surprised.

"My name is Camila," she said as she waved her hands around and two assistants came rushing over. "If you'd like to relax in the private lounge, we have champagne. Anything you need before I start showing you pieces?"

"No, no, I trust your judgment. *Completely*. But I really need to run some errands. Do you have a back entrance, somewhere I could sneak away for a bit?"

She winked at me. Actually winked. "We pride ourselves on our discretion."

"So I've heard," I murmured as she showed me to a back door that lead to an alleyway full of reeking garbage and other ancient smells. "This is perfect."

She raised her expertly sculpted brow.

"If anyone asks, just tell them I'm in the dressing room. And take your time . . . like . . . hours."

"Do you have sunglasses?"

"No, why?"

"If you're planning on going unnoticed, I think you'll need a pair. Your eyes are very distinctive," she said as she ducked inside, coming back with a pair of designer shades.

"I'll bring them back," I said.

"I know you will," she said, flashing Dane's credit card. This woman was slick.

Putting on the sunglasses, I sprinted down the alleyway, trying to look for any kind of monument so I could get my bearings.

I glanced at a clock in a nearby square. I had fifteen minutes to get to the café.

Following the bulk of the tourists, they led me to the Ramblas and from there I knew where I needed to go.

People were staring as I passed, gawking even. I didn't think I looked that different from everyone else. I was wearing black jeans and a blouse with a fitted blazer and flats. Maybe it was the fancy sunglasses.

As I rounded the corner, I let out a huge sigh of relief when I saw Timmons sitting at the café.

"Thank God you're okay," he blurted when he saw me. "I was just plotting how I was going to get you away from a heavily armed castle. What happened? I tried texting you and never heard back."

"Lucinda," I said as I sat down next to him. "I think she found my phone and took it."

"Ash, she's not to be tangled with."

"I'm getting that loud and clear, but what did you find out?"

"Not only were Coronado and Lucinda brother and sister, *twins*, but they were also lovers—"

"What?" I hunched over as if I'd been struck in the gut. "They're *twins*?"

"I didn't think that was the shocking part of the equation, but yes."

That's why Lucinda seemed so familiar to me. She looked like Coronado. The same brow, the same refined, but stern features. No wonder she acted so strangely when I spoke of my brother. And in her room, the etching of Coronado as a young man. Lucinda telling Beth a scary story about her brother . . . about true love. Dane had to have known about this.

"Ash, you really need to focus. Did anyone follow you here?" he asked.

"Dane sent guards with me, but I think they're back at the lingerie shop."

"Lingerie shop?"

"Forget it." I felt a flush spread to my cheeks.

A girl stepped in front of the table, giggled, and then snapped a photo of me with her cell phone.

"What the hell's going on?" I asked.

"This," he said as he slid a local paper in my direction. Front page. A photo of me and Dane from the Patrons Ball in New York City.

Mystery woman revealed!

Meet Ash Larkin, the average girl from New York City who's stolen billionaire playboy Dane Coronado's heart.

And there was another picture of my brother and me.

Her twin brother, Rhys Larkin, couldn't be reached for comment, but her classmates at Broughton Hall said she and her brother were inseparable and that she was an excellent lacrosse player.

Here are the results to the online poll: 32% are in favor of this Cinderella story, while 68% think he deserves better.

All I could think was that I left Dane alone at the estate and they knew. They knew who I was. That the immortal killer was my brother, my twin. "I have to warn Dane about this. If they see this, if they know, he's in as much danger as I am—maybe more."

"Unfortunately, that's the least of our problems."

"What do you mean?"

"Lucinda. She's the one who leaked your identity to the press."

"Conniving bitch," I said as I studied the paper.

A waiter came over to our table, placing espressos in front of us. "*Gaudeix.*"

"Bless you," Timmons replied, taking a huge gulp. "I thought you didn't want me drinking too much caffeine, but I'm not complaining. Good looking out."

I took a sip. "I didn't ask for it. Maybe they remembered your order from last time."

Looking around for the waiter, I caught a glimpse of him taking off his apron and walking briskly across the square. It took me a second to process where I knew him from, but I recognized his profile. It was the same guard from the castle who looked away from me when he was carrying the blood bags to the ballroom. The guard who'd come to Lucinda's room. The guard who'd found Max Pinter's body.

"Timmons, I don't know wh—"

When I turned back, there was a trail of blood streaming from Timmons's nostril. "Are you okay?"

He put his napkin to his nose to stop it, but then the blood started seeping from his eye sockets, his mouth, his pores. He grabbed the file in front of him, shoving it into my hands before he toppled to the ground.

"Oh God, no! Timmons, no!" I said as I crouched over him.

"The plans," he gurgled from his blood-filled mouth.

As I reached up to grab a butter knife from the table so I could cut open my wrist to try to save him, an Arcanum guard appeared out of nowhere, lifting me to my feet. "Mr. Coronado needs you," he said as he hurried me away from the square to a car waiting in an alleyway.

But as we got closer, Lucinda emerged from the backseat. "I've just come from the alchemist. I'm the only person who can help you now."

I dug in my heels as the guard tried to force me in the car. Jabbing my elbow into his ribs, I slipped out of his grasp and ran as fast as I could through swarms of tourists, weaving in and out of narrow streets. I was trying to figure out what to do, where to go, when I caught the scent of Dane's blood, along with the overwhelming stench of death.

"No," I whispered. "Not Dane."

30

LOCKING ON TO Dane's scent, I ran until I hit a dead end.

I was standing in front of the apothecary. The same place Lucinda said she'd just been. No lights were on. There was no welcome sign. But the scent of Dane's blood was everywhere.

With each step forward, the darkness inside of me raged, like a crow trapped inside my rib cage, battling for release.

As I opened the door, the scent hit me like a tidal wave. Dane was slumped over a body, black blood seeping into the grooves of the light wood floors, sprawling out like roots. As if it were reaching out for me.

"Dane," I gasped.

He didn't answer, but when I saw his shoulders tremble, I rushed toward him.

"I tried to save him, but it didn't work."

I looked down at the alchemist, who had black blood oozing from every orifice.

"I thought I might be able to heal him, the way you healed Beth."

"Dane." I turned his face toward mine. "Why would you think that? Why are you here?"

"I followed Lucinda." He clenched his jaw. "She killed him."

"I know. She killed Timmons, too," I said, desperately trying to hold it together for both of our sakes. "I was with him when he died . . . at the café."

"The café? Wait," he said in alarm. "Did *you* eat or drink anything at the café?"

"I . . . I'm not sure."

"Think." He shook me.

I was trying to remember, trying to picture anything other than Timmons's bleeding out, but I didn't need to remember—I could taste the coffee on my lips. "The waiter brought us coffee, but it wasn't a waiter. It was one of your guards. Lucinda's—"

"Pino. I knew they were close, but I had no idea she'd dragged him into this. Did you both drink it?"

"Yes. I had a sip, but I don't see how that matters. You know Rhys's blood won't affect me."

He dragged his fingers through his hair, looking completely distraught. "And now they know it, too. She wants to get rid of you, no matter the cost. Not only has your identity been revealed, but now they know you're immune. They'll want to drain you . . . use you however they see fit. They'll be coming for you."

"They already did. A guard tried to force me into Lucinda's car. She told me she'd seen the alchemist and that she was the only one who could help me. I ran—I caught the scent of your blood and death, and I thought—" I couldn't even finish the thought without breaking down in tears.

"I'm okay. We're together now," he said as he held me.

"Did you know Lucinda and Coronado were brother and sister?"

"You didn't know?"

"No . . . and they . . ."

"Believe me, I have the full picture. It's awful, but how did Lucinda even know about Timmons and Rennert? Where you would be?"

"She found a phone hidden in my room. The texts would have told her about my meeting with Timmons and about Rennert."

"You didn't trust me," he said, his eyes misting over.

"Timmons insisted. I'm sorry, I should've told you, but—"

Someone tapped on the front window, making me jump.

It was Dane's personal guard, the one who accompanied me to Barcelona. He entered, carrying a fresh set of clothes for Dane.

"Will you be okay for a moment?" he asked.

I nodded.

As Dane spoke with his guard and took a phone call, I couldn't help looking at Rennert, remembering everything he said to me . . . about twins and vessels, the light my mother gave to me, how I would have to give it away and step into darkness to find redemption. What did he mean? And now that he was gone, I was afraid I'd never find out.

I went to look for a tablecloth or a sheet to cover him with, when I noticed the blood-covered file spilled out across the floor. "Timmons," I whispered. I couldn't believe I forgot about that. Whatever was in there, I knew it was important. Important enough for him to shove it into my hands before dying.

Grabbing the file, I opened it to find a set of blueprints. *S. M. Residence* with a string of numbers printed on the top.

Laying them out on the counter, at first I thought maybe they were the same numbers I'd scrawled in the wax at the dinner party, but they were slightly off.

"What's this?" Dane asked as he draped the clothes over a chair, and washed his hands in a small copper sink.

"Timmons gave it to me," I said, sliding them over. "What does it mean? Why would he have these?"

"This is why," Dane said, pointing to a section of the drawing. "Here, below the ground level, there's a windowless room with a medical-grade air filtration system. This is the place."

"The plans." I swallowed hard. "*S. M.*, that could be for Spencer Mendoza."

"And look at the stamp," Dane said as he pointed to the *MP* stamp on the bottom. "That's Max Pinter's company logo."

"Pinter designed this?" I asked. "He was screaming, 'Look at the plans,' right before Lucinda called the guards on him. She must've known he was getting ready to confess."

Dane's brow furrowed in anguish. "He must've been trying

to come clean about his involvement in all this, and I sent him away. To be slaughtered."

"You couldn't have known," I said. "You were only trying to protect me. But where is this? There's no address."

Dane got out his phone and took a picture of the file number and sent it to someone. Along with a text, **I just sent you a file number. Max Pinter was the architect. I need the address of this project, ASAP.** "I have my best man on it," he said as he put his phone away. "We should have everything we need soon. We're going to find him." He took off his bloodstained shirt to change into a fresh one his guard brought. I tried not to look, but I couldn't help myself.

"In the meantime, I have a plan," he said as he slowly fastened the buttons. "But I need to know that you trust me."

He had me at a bit of a disadvantage, but Dane had been nothing but forthright with me since I arrived in Spain. I made a decision to clear the slate, give him another chance, but in order to do that, I needed to step off the precipice and let him prove to be my equal.

"I trust you," I said.

I felt a sense of relief rush through him, through me.

"I'll tell you everything, but first we need to get you cleaned up," he said.

"Why?"

"All you need to know is that by tomorrow morning, you, me, Beth, and Rhys will all be together, and nothing—I mean nothing—will get in our way again."

31

BY THE TIME we returned to the lingerie store, it was swarming with paparazzi.

"We need to get out of here," I said as I sank down in the backseat of Dane's car.

"No. This is exactly what we want. There's nothing the council hates more than publicity, but Lucinda's not the only one with media connections," Dane said as he put on his cuff links.

"You did this?"

"We're making a statement."

I glanced down at the blood on my clothes, smeared all over my hands and neck. "But look at me—"

"Already taken care of. While I distract them out front, my driver will take you around back. I have people waiting inside. They know what to do."

"Dane," I said as I squeezed his hand.

"You can do this," he assured me as he arranged my hair

around my shoulders, giving me a breathless kiss full of blood and sorrow, lust and remorse, and all I wanted to do in that moment was to give myself over and get lost in him, but he pulled away, emerging from the car with a broad smile on his face.

It brought a lump to my throat, watching him work the crowd. He was putting everything on the line for my brother and me. I didn't really deserve his devotion, especially after the way I'd behaved with Coronado, but we were going to have to lean on each other to get through this. To get Rhys back.

The driver pulled around to the alleyway. The door unlocked, and it startled me. As much as I wanted to curl up in a ball and hide from the world, I took a deep breath and got out of the car, running to the back door of the shop. I had to be brave for Dane . . . for Rhys.

The moment I stepped inside, Camila introduced me to a team of stylists, and I was rushed to the bathroom. They took off my clothes, threw them in the trash, and then they washed me up. No questions asked.

They went to work on my hair and makeup. Normally, I would've hated this much attention, this much fuss, but I was in a daze. I was so tired of fighting everything all the time— fighting my feelings for Dane, fighting my fear about Rhys, fighting the other immortals—and the truth was I couldn't do this alone.

They dressed me in a nude balconette bra with matching panties and a cream-colored fitted tank dress with a pair of beige heels and a jeweled clutch. When they were finished, I looked in the mirror and realized this was what a Dane Coronado love interest should look like. Polished and buffed to perfection.

After piling up exquisitely wrapped boxes into the two Arcanum guards' arms, Camila handed me a small bag with their logo prominently displayed. I got it. It was a nice plug for their store. And God only knows how much Dane had to fork over for this degree of discretion, but I was grateful. "Oh, your sunglasses," I said as I started to give them back, but she placed them firmly on my face.

"Keep them. They look better on you anyway."

"Thank you."

"Don't worry. It's reflected in the bill," she said as she tucked his credit card and a receipt as long as my body length inside the bag. "Little tip," she whispered. "When you reach the bottom of the stairs, take off the glasses. They'll want to see those eyes."

All I could do was nod.

As she stepped outside to open the door, the cameras started flashing.

The guards hurried out, deftly maneuvering through the crowd.

As I stood on the threshold, I took in a jittery breath. It felt symbolic, as if stepping over this threshold meant that I was choosing to embrace Dane Coronado and everything that came with him.

I wasn't sure if someone nudged me or if I took the first step, but as soon as I emerged into the open air, a barrage of flashes and questions awaited me.

I focused on Dane, who was waiting for me at the foot of the stairs. And that's all I needed. I breathed him in, focused on his emotions, leaning on his confidence, his love, his strength to get me through this.

As soon as I reached his side, Dane slid his arm around my waist. "Just smile," he whispered. "We're nearly there."

He kissed my cheek and turned to the reporters. "This is the woman I've been telling you about. May I present Miss Ashlyn Marie Larkin."

The sound of cameras clicking, pens scribbling on paper, made my head spin.

"How does it feel having the attention of the most eligible bachelor in the world?" a reporter asked.

"Are you planning a trip?"

"Are there wedding bells in your future?"

"I certainly hope so." Dane grinned. "Believe me, it's not from a lack of trying. You'll put in a good word for me, I hope?"

The reporters laughed. He was so charming, so effortless. I guess he'd had a year to practice. I couldn't imagine how difficult that must've been for him. He was forced into the limelight from day one, while a war was being waged inside of him. And he still managed somehow. The least I could do was stand here and smile.

The woman from the shop was waving at me from the stairs, reminding me to take off my sunglasses.

The flashes went crazy.

"Where did you meet?"

"Does your family approve? What about your twin brother?"

"It was love at first sight," Dane offered in an attempt to deflect the questions. "At least on my part, but I think I'm starting to grow on her."

"Is that true, Miss Larkin? Is he starting to win you over with lavish shopping trips?"

Dane squeezed my hand. He knew that would set me off. I could make enough gold in a month to buy this store out ten times over, but I strangled the thought.

"And how do you know all of this isn't for me?" Dane grinned. "Now, if you'll excuse us," he said as he motioned for me to get in the car. "As you can see, we have more pressing matters to attend to."

A low chuckle swept through the crowd as he slipped in next to me and shut the door on the world.

32

"L'ACADÈMIA," DANE SAID to the driver.

He took the sunglasses and bag from my trembling hands. "You were perfect," he said, lacing his fingers through mine.

His touch was an anchor holding me to myself, reminding me that I wasn't alone in this. There was no denying the connection we had, but it was beyond blood at this point. It was a shared experience, something I could never explain to another living soul. We'd been through so much together. He knew me probably better than I knew myself. And for the first time, I felt like I knew him, too. All of him. Including Coronado. And I was strangely at peace with that.

He wrapped his arms around me and I didn't feel stifled, only loved and protected.

The car pulled up to a narrow street and we got out. Arcanum guards were lining the alleyway, along with the paparazzi.

"This is a message from the council," Dane said in a low

voice. "They're watching, but fortunately for us, so is the rest of the world."

We strolled hand in hand up the winding, narrow cobblestone path to a small square, brimming with life.

There was a small medieval chapel tucked between a café with bright red chairs clustered around a handful of small tables and an art gallery with apartments above. Clothes hung from lines strung from balcony to balcony. The Catalan flag in full display. Gauzy drapes fluttering in the gentle breeze. Flowerpots and cats in windowsills, guitar music wafting through the air.

Dane led me to a restaurant called L'Acadèmia, nestled between two ancient buildings, directly across from the chapel. It was small and rustic. The dark wood interior gleamed in candlelight. But it was empty. I was about to ask him where everyone was when I saw him slip a stack of cash into the owner's hand. A short, stocky waiter in starched linens showed us to a cozy banquette in the corner of the room. Dane and I sat next to each other, so we could gaze out at the square, and so the paparazzi could look in at us. Whatever the case, the seating arrangement made it easy to whisper in each other's ears.

The waiter brought over a bottle of champagne. It looked old. Dane inspected the bottle, then gave a nod of approval.

The cork popped and the waiter poured two glasses, being extremely careful not to waste a single drop.

"I thought you never eat or drink in public places."

Dane raised his glass. "None of that matters now."

We clinked glasses and took a sip.

"This is nice, but how is it a part of the plan?" I whispered in his ear.

He took my hand, stroking his thumb against my palm. Just that slight touch made me catch my breath.

"We're closing in on Spencer," he whispered back. "Thanks to Timmons's research, we should have the location within the hour."

He must've felt a wave of sadness pass over me, because he raised his glass. "To Timmons."

Blinking back the tears, I clinked his glass and took another sip.

"What are we doing here? Shouldn't we be preparing?"

"We are. I have three things to deal with at the moment. First is bringing Rhys home safely to you and Beth. The jet is ready to go. I have a team in place. Medical assistance at the ready. Hazmat suits. We are prepared for every possible scenario.

"Second, it seems I have a hostile takeover happening in my own house. Lucinda is the ringleader, but there may be others. Those Arcanum guards lining the street, they were sent for a reason. To escort us back to the castle, where they will promptly drain you, before ordering our immurement. I'll need to find a way to satisfy them in order to put a stop to this. And then I'll be able to deal with the traitors accordingly.

"And third, but certainly not last," he said as he arranged my hair around my shoulders, "I need to protect you."

"Oh, that's all," I said with an uncomfortable laugh.

The waiter refilled our glasses.

"I think I've found a way I can do all three things in one fell swoop."

"How?"

"Your blood. If we can offer them your blood, I believe we can make a deal."

"You want them to bleed me out?"

"No. A drop each will do."

"I don't understand. I had to give Beth *liters* of my blood to save her, and that was a close call. There's no way a drop of blood would be able to protect them against the effects of Rhys's blood—"

"To save someone, yes. But your blood isn't just a cure for the effects of Rhys's blood. It's also a vaccination."

"What? How do you know?"

"Last night, I was reviewing the security footage from my office, and I saw Lucinda place a drop from the amulet she wears around her neck into my tea when I wasn't looking. She stood there and smiled as she watched me drink it. She tried to kill me, but it was your blood coursing through my veins that saved me. If we could offer the immortals protection, they'd have nothing to fear."

"And what's to stop them from taking my blood—immuring us—and still killing my brother?"

"That's where all of this comes in," he said as he waved at the cameras lined up outside. "We are going to create a media frenzy. If we disappeared, not even the council would be able to buy their way out of the attention. They won't be able to touch us."

"And when the media frenzy dies?"

"Trust me. After tonight, we won't have to worry about the council ever again." He leaned in, brushing his lips against my ear. "We make our peace offering, and while they're vacating the premises, you and I will accompany a small team of my best men to Spencer's location, where we'll rescue your brother. And by the time we return to Castell de Coronado, the council will be gone, Lucinda will be dealt with, and you and me and Beth and Rhys can live happily ever after."

"But how are we going to create this media frenzy? Once they get their photo for the papers, they'll be gone."

He took a deep sip of his champagne before continuing. I could feel his nerves starting to fire. And before I could even process where he was going with all this, he took a knee.

"Miss Ashlyn Marie Larkin. Will you honor me with your hand in marriage?" He pulled a deep red leather box from his pocket, presenting me with a ring. Not just any ring. It was the gorgeous gray stone from his collection, set in a sea of diamonds.

Cameras started flashing through the front windows.

"Dane, I—"

"I'm asking you to take one more chance on me. Let me prove to be your equal every day for the rest of eternity. I will not let you down. This is how I can protect you, honor you, and keep you safe. We're already blood bound, which—to me—is more sacred than marriage, but let me legally bind to you, since that's the language that the world will understand. I want to give you my name. My power. My body. My soul."

I didn't know if it was Dane or the moment or the champagne, but I stretched out my hand, letting him slip the ring onto my finger.

I heard cheers from outside, a flood of cameras clicking, and bells from the church ringing.

"After you," he said as he stood, looking across the way at the church.

"Wait—what? Right n-now?" I stammered.

"Why not?"

"But I always thought Rhys would be with me. My man of honor. And Beth. Beth would die to see this. She loves us both so much."

"And we can do it all over again. And again and again. Every week, every decade, every lifetime. As often as you want." He pulled me into an embrace, whispering in my ear, "And maybe we can find a way to make Beth and Rhys immortal, too. The possibilities are endless."

I felt drunk with the notion. Maybe this was meant to be.

Dane had arranged everything—from the rings, to the flowers, to the marriage certificate, to the priest. The ceremony was a private affair, with just the Arcanum guards as our witnesses. I wasn't one of those girls who grew up fantasizing what her wedding would be like, but it certainly wasn't this. It felt cold and impersonal, a business arrangement, until Dane kissed me. The scent of crushed violets between us, his lips finding mine, the taste of champagne on the tip of his tongue, the warmth spreading through every part of me.

In blood, in body, in spirit, in holy matrimony, we were bound.

. . .

The ride back to the estate seemed surreal. The feel of the platinum and stone around my finger, the strange intimacy of what we just shared, paired with the anticipation of what we were about to walk into, proved to be an intoxicating mix.

I wanted to close the privacy screen and lose myself in him more than ever.

I kept waiting for Dane to make a move, but he never did. Instead, we went over the plan a hundred times, but it still felt like I was walking directly into a lion's den. Or lioness's den, to be exact. Lucinda had tried to kill me. Kill Dane. She'd murdered my lawyer. My friend. And somehow I had to face her without ripping her throat out. That was Dane's one condition. He didn't want to humiliate her in front of the council. He wanted to deal with her on his own, when this was all over. I understood why. She was Coronado's twin and former lover, but letting it go would be one of the hardest things I'd ever have to do.

Hand in hand, Dane and I walked down the long seashell path, bathed in moonlight. With a line of Arcanum guards pressing in behind us, we ascended the stairs, stepping into the main hall, to find all of the immortals standing there, waiting, a tense hush sucking all the air from the room.

"Liars," someone finally hissed.

"You've just sealed your immurement."

"Not today," Dane said. "You see, I've just released the guest list to our little wedding party. So, if anything happens to us, you'll have to answer to them," Dane said, pulling back the heavy drapes and waving to the sea of cameras crowded outside the gate.

"You think that will stop us?" Mr. Jaeger laughed. "Horrible accidents happen all the time."

"Before you start waving your pitchforks," Dane said, "we have something we'd like to share with you. Consider it our wedding gift to you." He nodded to one of his guards. "To show our commitment to peace, we'd like to offer each of you a drop of Ashlyn's blood."

"A-a drop?" Mr. Bridges sputtered. "We know from witnesses that it would take a hell of a lot more than that."

Mr. Jaeger took a step forward. "What do you take us for . . . fools?"

"Precisely, and if you interrupt me one more time, I'll slit your throat open . . . *again*."

Dane motioned to his personal guard, who brought over an IV and a blood bag. "Lucinda. Would you do the honors?"

She seemed unnerved, but he hadn't given her away as the person responsible for the immortal murders yet, so she played along. There seemed to be an understanding between the two of them, a connection I hadn't sensed before, but once I learned the truth about the nature of their relationship, it's all I could see. All I could feel. The longing. The depravity. The secrets.

As everyone watched, Lucinda jabbed the needle in my vein and drew blood into the bag.

Dane was focused on his guard. "Please go down to the cellar. Fetch two cases of '64 Dom." There was a split second of recognition that flashed between them—something I didn't completely understand, but I was so caught up in the energy around me that I couldn't distinguish his emotions from mine or Lucinda's or the pure bloodlust permeating the room. Everything was a jumbled mass of suspicion and hatred.

When the bag was full, Lucinda ripped the needle out, glaring down at the ring on my finger.

"We'll need two guards for the demonstration," Dane said as he took the blood bag from her. "I'll choose one and you choose one," he said to Lucinda. "To make it fair. How about Pino."

Lucinda's jaw clenched, but that was her only show of emotion. She wouldn't be able to object without giving herself away.

Having to stand there while Lucinda's guard walked past me, the same man who killed Timmons just a few hours ago, was excruciating.

But I could feel Dane's blood searing through his veins. This was hard for him, too.

"Bennett," Lucinda called out.

One of Dane's key guards.

As the guards stepped forward, Dane took a glass from a servant's tray and dripped some of my blood inside. He then handed the blood bag to the guard who'd brought up the champagne and turned to Lucinda, inconspicuously ripping the amulet from her neck.

"We were able to procure a vial of the immortal killer's blood from a certain nefarious alchemist," Dane said as he showed it to everyone.

"Rennert," I heard people whisper.

It hurt that Dane was putting the blame on Rennert, but I understood why. If the immortal council knew that Lucinda was the one behind this, they would shred her to pieces on the spot and immure her in the bowels of the earth. Dane couldn't do that to Coronado. Evil or not, I understood the bond between twins.

"Now, which one of you would like to try Miss Larkin's blood first?"

Neither guard spoke up, but Dane went ahead. "Excellent choice, Bennett. You may go first," Dane said as he topped off the glass containing a drop of my blood with champagne, swishing it around in the glass for all of them to see, before handing it to him.

"To life."

The guard raised the glass to his trembling lips and drank it in one shot.

"And how do you feel?" Dane asked.

"Fine, sir." The guard seemed to stand a little taller.

"Now for the not-so-fun part," Dane said as he took another glass and handed it to Lucinda. "You're so good at this, why don't you show us how it's done?"

Reluctantly, she stepped forward, taking the amulet from him. With trembling hands, she did as she was instructed, placing a drop in the second glass. Dane topped it off with champagne and motioned for her to give it to Pino.

As she handed it to him, I saw her brush his fingers tenderly; I saw her lips moving, possibly a prayer for his soul.

His eyes glossy with tears, Pino lifted his glass and drank it, never looking away from Lucinda.

Within seconds, the guard's nose started bleeding, then blood was gushing from every orifice. The members of the council stepped back, covering their mouths, horrified by the carnage.

Bennett, the guard who ingested my blood first, stood there shell-shocked, but relieved.

"Now, a drop of the killer's blood for Bennett," Dane called to Lucinda.

"But won't that kill him? Doesn't he need to drink more of her blood first?" one of the council members asked.

The crowd erupted in panicked whispers, but I couldn't make out what they were saying . . . thinking.

Lucinda carefully measured out a drop in Bennett's glass, then Dane came up behind her, grabbing hold of her hand. "Hell, let's do the whole thing," he said as he tipped the amulet, filling the bottom of the glass with Rhys's deathly blood.

"Go on," Dane said to his guard.

Bennett cringed as he tipped the glass, filling his mouth with blood. We watched him swallow . . . we waited . . . and waited . . . but nothing happened.

The crowd was agitated, but in a good way. Abuzz with the idea of what a drop of my blood could do.

"As you can see, Ashlyn's blood is not only the cure, it's the vaccination. One drop and the immortal killer is no longer a threat to you."

"What's in it for you?" Mr. Davenport asked.

"Other than your word that no one will make a move against us, we ask that you let us handle the boy in our own way. Without interference."

"And let you control the most deadly poison in the world?" Mr. Jaeger said. "I think not."

"You have my word that he'll be secured until his natural death. His blood will never be harvested as a weapon."

"Your word?" Mr. Jaeger laughed.

"Then how about *my* word?" I said as I stood next to Dane. "My brother's blood was being stolen from him. He would never consent to hurt a living soul. Even you. I'm willing to bet my freedom on it. If my brother's blood is responsible for another death, you have my permission to come for me."

"Do we have an accord?" Dane asked.

One by one, the council members shook Dane's hand, slapped him on the back, and kissed his cheeks, as if all were forgiven.

Dane announced, "When you're ready, there will be private jets, cars, boats, whatever you need, so you can return to your lives. And we'll meet again next year, under much happier circumstances. But for now," he said as he held his arms out wide, "all I ask is that you toast to our marriage."

As the glasses were handed out, an excited rush of emotions swept through the crowd.

Dane nodded to his personal guard to place a drop of blood from the blood bag into each glass. "Make sure all the other guards get a glass. You too." He smiled warmly at Lucinda.

"Now, if you'll excuse us," Dane said as he swooped me up

in his arms, "I've been waiting over four hundred years for this night."

Everyone cheered and congratulated us as he carried me up the grand staircase.

"Was that too much?" Dane whispered in my ear. "I think that's how Coronado would've handled it."

"I believed every word," I said as I nuzzled into his neck.

I couldn't help thinking of the last time Dane carried me like this. I was naked, covered in blood, when he carried me out of the corn and into the lake. It felt exactly the same, like it was us against the world all over again.

Dane opened the door to my bedroom. "Are you ready?" he asked as he threw me onto the bed.

"Ready for what?" I replied with a shallow breath.

"To rescue your brother. I just got word. He's in Madrid." He grinned down at me. "What did you think I meant?"

I pushed myself up on my elbows. "Nothing, I just—"

"We may be married, but this time, you'll need to come to me," he said as he traced a pattern on my ankle with his thumb. "When you're ready, I want you to unlock the door between our chambers. I want no barriers between us. No doubts."

As I sat there trying to catch my breath, he grabbed a pair of black jeans, a black T-shirt, and some sneakers from the armoire, placing them on the bed.

"I assume you'll want to check on Beth before we go," he said.

"Yes," I replied, desperately trying to pull my thoughts out of the gutter.

"I'll meet you there," he said as he slipped out of my room and went into his own room to change.

Before I could even give myself a chance to contemplate removing the key from the agate box, I dressed and snuck across the breezeway. There was plenty of time for all that. Eternity, to be exact.

I nodded to the guards, and when I opened Beth's door, I found her crouched on the floor, her ear to the ground.

"Beth? Are you okay?" I asked as I sat next to her.

"Yes," she answered in a daze as she sat up. "I'm just trying to piece things together."

"I have the best news," I said as I took her hands. "We found Rhys. We're going to get him right now and bring him back here."

"Back?" she asked.

"The other immortals are leaving. They'll be gone by the time we return. It's going to be the four of us, just like your vision. If you can make some snow happen by the time we come back, that would be great."

"Ash, I—"

Dane appeared in the doorway. "Are you ready, Mrs. Dane Mendoza Coronado?"

"I'll be keeping my name, thank you very much."

"What?" Beth inhaled sharply.

"It's true," I said as I showed her my ring. "We got married. I know it's crazy, but it's certainly not the craziest thing I've done with this man."

Beth smiled, but it was strained. I thought she'd be ecstatic, but maybe she was just disappointed that we didn't include her, or maybe it was cabin fever.

"We should go," Dane said.

"Soon, this will all be over," I said as I squeezed her hands. "The next time you see me, I'll be with Rhys."

"I know," she whispered.

With the sound of revelry and corks popping in the background, we snuck out a side entrance and into the night air, a team of six of Dane's closest guards waiting for us.

When I looked back at the castle, I saw a figure in the tower window. It was Beth.

Only this time, she didn't wave.

33

WE DROVE TO a nearby airstrip, boarding a private jet to Madrid. Dane's team of guards was swift and thorough, attending to every detail. Clearly, they'd been well trained. As soon as we were airborne, they went straight to work on setting up a quarantine section in the back of the plane: a boxy frame covered with thick, clear plastic sheeting.

They were under strict instructions not to come into direct contact with my brother's blood. It made me uncomfortable, but we had no idea what condition he would be in, and the last thing Rhys needed was additions to the body count. I kept thinking about the alchemist talking about twins and vessels, giving away my light. Maybe that had something to do with how I could help my brother.

As if reading my thoughts, Dane wrapped his arm around me. "We'll have medical assistance standing by, whatever he needs—"

"It's not necessary." I shook my head. "My blood. I'll give him my blood. That should seal any open wounds." The thought made me woozy. Rhys hated blood. I couldn't imagine anything worse for him than being trapped and drugged for a year while they slowly drained him.

"We should go over the mission," Dane said as he led me to the front of the plane, where food and drinks had been set out. But I wasn't hungry. I wasn't thirsty. There was a pit in my stomach that I hadn't felt since Dane and I walked into the corn for the last time. But I wasn't walking to my doom this time. I was going to rescue my brother. I pushed the darker thoughts out of my head. Beth saw us together. I had to believe this was going to be okay.

"This is where we'll enter," Dane said as he spread a full set of blueprints out on the table.

Spencer Mendoza Residence was listed on the top with *Max Pinter, Architect* listed beneath.

"Where will Rhys be?" I asked as I studied the plans.

"We think he'll be in this area." Dane pointed to the windowless room, beneath a small dining room off the kitchen. "The access point should be here somewhere, although there's no door listed in the plans. But we know the room exists."

I traced the outline of the room with my fingertip, trying to imagine what it was going to be like seeing him again after all this time. But then I thought of Dane. "How do you feel about seeing your parents?" I whispered.

"Angry. Hurt. Right after the solstice, Spencer reached out

227

to me—thinking I was Coronado. He didn't care that his son was dead. All he wanted was money. I think that's when he and Lucinda must've struck a deal. Because when I refused to give him the money Coronado had promised, this is what he did. I can't help thinking that maybe I could've stopped all of this."

"It isn't your fault." I took his hand in mine. His thumb lingered on the platinum band of my ring.

"Probably not your ideal wedding night," he said as he looked around at the men putting on their hazmat gear.

"It's kind of perfect for us." I let out a burst of nervous laughter. "But finding Rhys," I said as I squeezed his hand tight. "That's the best wedding gift I could possibly ask for."

I looked down at the ring, the gray stone glittering like a tiny universe made for Dane and me, and I hoped Rhys would want to be a part of that. I hoped he could accept Dane . . . accept us.

As if Dane knew what I was thinking, he stroked my cheek. "Together, we can conquer anything."

The moment we landed on a private airstrip outside of Madrid, we were whisked away in a black van. Dane and I sat in the front, while the rest of the team rode in the back, loading ammo into their guns, putting bulletproof vests over their hazmat suits.

"Is that really necessary?" I asked.

"We have no idea what we're walking into. It could be a trap. The way they're imprisoning Rhys . . . if we're not careful, they could do the same thing to us."

"But what if they shoot Rhys by mistake?"

"What's rule number one?" Dane called out to his men.

"The boy will not be harmed under any circumstances," they answered back with military precision.

They handed Dane a hazmat suit, but he refused. "It's more than just your blood protecting me. Even if he wanted to harm me, he wouldn't. We're family now."

God, I hoped that was true. The last time my brother saw Dane, he tried to hit him, and that was before he even knew the truth about what Dane did to me, did to our family.

The closer we got to the blue dot on the GPS, the more apprehensive I became. Everything in the past year had led me to this moment. Dane held my hand. He didn't say anything. We didn't need to. We were both a tangled-up mass of nerves and emotion.

As we pulled up in front of a house, the men put on their night-vision goggles. The house was dark, the windows boarded up. There was a construction sign out front with Max Pinter's logo on it.

"Stay alert. Do not harm the boy," Dane said to his men.

At precisely two a.m., we emerged from the van, silently moving toward the front of the house. I was expecting them to bash down the door, but they put some kind of device into the locks, which opened them right up. As soon as we entered the house, I nearly gagged on the stench of eucalyptus and blood. My brother's mixed with someone else's. It was so fresh I could taste it, but cutting through it all was the acrid scent of fear. It was everywhere, practically suffocating me.

The men swept the house, homing in on an interior room with the soft flicker of candlelight seeping out from under the door. It was eerily quiet. Just the sound of heavy breath along with a low, painfully slow drip.

One of the guards showed us the thermal image reading. It looked like there were two people in the room. One image was so weak it hardly showed up on the screen. The other was strong and angry, almost pulsing through the screen.

Dane looked at me and I nodded. He gave the signal; the guards kicked in the door, guns aimed and ready to fire.

Dane and I stepped in to find a stark room furnished with only a farm table and two chairs. Teresa and Spencer were seated on either end, with a single lit candle between them. Teresa was slumped over the table, clutching an empty glass, her eyes wide, blood seeping from her eye sockets, nose, and mouth, funneling into the cracks of the wood, before dripping to the floor. She reeked of my brother's blood.

Spencer sat there, at the opposite end of the table, his hands gripping the cup of red liquid in front of him.

"Should we call for medical?" one of the guards asked.

Dane shook his head. He looked furious. I'd never felt such hatred and fear pouring out of him. He crossed to Teresa, placing his hand on her neck, feeling for a pulse. He clenched his jaw as he closed Teresa's eyes.

"Where's Rhys?" I asked.

Spencer didn't answer. The only movement was the bead of

sweat trailing down the side of his face, disappearing under his chin. "I know we were supposed to drink at the same time," he murmured. "But something stopped me. I knew, I just knew—"

"I'll deal with him," Dane interrupted. I could feel him trying to keep control of his emotions. "Find Rhys. There should be an entry point in this room. Is there a false wall?"

"I've located a possible entry device," one of the guards called out as he slid the cover off a fake electrical socket. Dane dug a set of keys out of Spencer's pocket and slid them across the table. But still, Spencer didn't move. It was as if he were frozen in fear.

As soon as the guard found the right key, the wall popped open.

The stale scent of my brother's blood, saline, and iodine flooded my nostrils.

Fluorescent lights pinged to life, casting an unnatural glow on the concrete walls of the hidden chamber.

I descended the stairs, calling out Rhys's name, but my heart sank when I reached the bottom only to find a makeshift hospital room with no one in it. There was a hospital bed, IVs, blood pumps, syringes, gauze, bandages, morphine . . . everything one would need to keep someone prisoner for a year of bloodletting, but no Rhys.

Heavy canvas straps dangled from the sides of the hospital bed. There was dried blood on the sheets. As I pushed the fabric to my face, taking in a deep whiff, the guards took a step back, breathing into their respirators. "He was here," I whispered. "Do you see what this means?" I lay down on the hospital bed, reenacting it, seeing what he saw, trying to feel what he felt. "He must've gotten ahold of something sharp," I said as I inspected the restraints. They'd been cut.

"And look, this blood spatter on the floor must've happened when he ripped out his IV." I followed the drops of blood to a utility closet filled with cleaning supplies, fresh scrubs, and linens. "Maybe he grabbed a pair of scrubs." I then followed the few random drops leading back up the stairs. "He must've escaped," I said to Dane as I reentered the room. "How long has my brother been gone?" I demanded an answer from Spencer.

Dane kicked his chair. "I've tried, but he won't say another word. Maybe he's still trying to protect Lucinda."

"Please." My voice quivered. "Rhys is my twin. He's the only family I have left," I said as I gripped the edge of the table. "I need to find him."

Spencer finally met my eyes and it took me aback. His face was full of despair, remorse and pity—he seemed nothing like the arrogant man I remembered. "You should know . . . you should know the truth. He's not who you—"

Dane snatched a knife from one of the guard's belts.

"Please, don't. No, Coronado, not like this," Spencer screamed.

Dane plunged the blade into Spencer's neck.

As Spencer's blood painted the walls, the guards stepped back, watching Dane unleash a fury like I'd never seen before. But it wasn't Dane anymore. He stabbed him again and again and again.

"Dane," I said as I grabbed his blood-spattered face, forcing him to look at me.

232

Tears sprang to his eyes, and his hands began to tremble.

"Leave us," I yelled at the guards. As they filed from the room, I pried the knife out of Dane's hands.

"I did this?" he whispered.

"It wasn't you."

"You don't understand. I let Coronado take over, completely. I couldn't face it. After everything my father did to me, everything he did to you, and now Rhys . . ." He glanced at what was left of Spencer, then back to his bloody hands. "But look what I've done," he said as he crumpled to the floor. "I killed my own father."

"I know." I clutched his blood-drenched hands in mine.

As I sat with him, nestled between a pool of his mother's blood . . . his father's blood, my first instinct was to wrap my arms around him, tell him it was going to be okay. But none of this was ever going to be okay. I didn't wipe away his tears. I didn't wipe away the evidence. He needed to do that himself. When he was ready.

This was something he'd have to live with for the rest of his life—better to face it now. Head-on. Blood and all.

"I let Coronado take over because, on some level, this is what I wanted. But I was too weak to do it myself."

"You are anything but weak. You came back to me. That's all that matters."

"Rhys . . ." His chin began to quiver. "I promised you—"

"And you will keep that promise." I held him firm. "For all we know, Rhys could be on his way to the estate right now. He's alive. He's out there. I can feel it. We're going to find him."

I stood, taking it all in. I wasn't sorry they were dead. Teresa was finally at peace, and Spencer finally got what he deserved. I would've liked to have gotten some answers out of him before he died, but Dane had his own reasons . . . his own demons to contend with.

"Let's go home," I said as I pulled him to his feet. "Tomorrow we'll regroup. Start again."

He looked up at me, his eyes so full of anguish and promise that it made my heart ache. This was the Dane I remembered. This was the Dane I wanted.

We'd both killed a parent. We'd both been possessed by our ancestors. We'd both been pulled back from the brink by love.

If he wasn't my equal, I didn't know what was.

And if he could be redeemed . . . so could I.

34

WE WERE SILENT the entire plane ride back to Castell de Coronado.

The benefit and the curse of being blood bound was that I knew exactly what he was feeling. Sadness, fear, exhaustion, but it was the guilt that overwhelmed me. I understood it better than anyone. He was embarrassed for showing weakness around me, but he didn't need to be. In that moment, his trembling hands covered in blood, I'd never felt closer to him, more bound to him.

It was just before dawn when we arrived back at the estate.

We used the side entrance to avoid seeing anyone, but the castle was quiet, empty. I was grateful. For me, for Dane, for everything we'd been through over the past twenty-four hours.

The scent of fresh blood, Pino's decaying corpse, and fragrant white flowers from the champagne was undeniable. No doubt the immortals had some kind of blood orgy to celebrate their victory before returning to their empty lives. The good news was that I'd have an entire year to prepare for their next visit. Hopefully, a much shorter visit.

When we reached the top of the stairs, I told Dane I needed to speak with Beth, tell her what happened.

He nodded and went to his room. It was the hardest thing, watching him slink into the dark, alone. But he needed some time to come to terms with what happened.

On my way to Beth's room, I practiced what I was going to say to her, but nothing sounded right. I was relieved to see the guards were gone from their post. The door to her room was left slightly ajar, but the lights were off.

I knocked lightly. "Beth," I whispered. "It's Ash."

When she didn't reply, I took it as a sign. Let her have one more night of sweet dreams. One more night of thinking that when she woke, Rhys would be by her side.

One more night wouldn't hurt any of us.

Going back to my room, I took off my bloodstained clothes and looked at myself in the mirror. I no longer saw a girl haunted by memories, I saw a woman.

I knew Dane. He knew me. All our strengths, all our weaknesses.

In sickness and in health.

Tonight I was putting aside all the artifice, all the posturing, all the walls. And I was going to live in the moment. With Dane.

I brushed out my hair, put on a dab of lip balm, and slipped on the white silk robe.

Opening the agate box on my bedside table, I felt the weight of the key in my hand and everything it meant. Sliding it into the lock, I opened the door and stepped inside the darkened room.

Dane was crouched in front of the fire, a towel wrapped around his waist, his gorgeous olive skin dotted with beads of water from the shower. He didn't even register me coming in; his eyes were trained on the fire, no doubt replaying the carnage he'd just inflicted on an endless loop.

I knew that pain. Better than anyone.

The air was thick with regret, which only seemed to intensify his scent of sandalwood, musk, and earth. The pain pouring off of him was all consuming. I remembered what that was like— walking out of the corn, watching the sun come up on endless days of loss and regret—and I wanted to ease his pain. I wanted him to pour that sadness into me so I could share the burden.

"Love is love no matter how it comes to you," I said as I stepped behind him. "I understand that now more than ever."

"Forgive me," he said as he glanced back at me. "I'll get dressed."

"There's no need," I replied.

I'd always thought it was impossible to tell what color Dane's eyes were—blue, green, or gold—but that's exactly how Dane was: complicated. But there was nothing complicated about this. About being with him in this way. It was actually the simplest thing in the world. And all I had to do was show him that this is what I wanted. That I was ready.

I handed him the key.

He glanced toward the door, surprised to find it open.

"I come to you with no barriers between us," I said as I untied the robe, letting it drop to the floor. "Everything I have is yours."

I watched him take me in. I welcomed it.

As he stood to face me, he tossed the key into the fire.

Skimming my fingers across the edge of the towel wrapped around his waist, I pulled it free. It dropped to the floor with a heavy thud. I smoothed my hands across his chest, and his breath shuddered. As I moved in close, pressing my body against his, running my fingers over his shoulder blades, I felt a change come over him—the sadness washed away by passion. I nuzzled my face into his neck, my lips brushing a pulsing vein. Suddenly, I wanted to feel the rush of his blood pulsing through mine. I longed for the closeness we felt under Heartbreak Tree. And I wanted to show him that I would've made the same choice. In any lifetime, in any form, I would choose him all over again.

I took the letter opener from his desk and slit the palm of his hand and then my own. We laced our fingers together. The feel of his blood entering my bloodstream was euphoric. Everything I remembered, but it was so much more complex now. Time had only intensified my feelings, my desire to be with him in this way. As our wounds healed shut, a completely different desire rose up inside of me.

As if reading my thoughts, he glanced toward the bed.

"A little conventional for us, wouldn't you say?"

A sly smile tugged at the corner of his mouth before he shoved the coffee table out of the way and we tumbled to the ground.

The cold marble against my skin, the heat from the flames of the fire licking our backs, his mouth all over me, mine all over him. The desire consuming us from the outside in. He placed his hands firmly on my bare hips, stopping any movement.

"We have all the time in the world," he whispered. "This is not only our wedding night, but the first night of the rest of our lives. Eternity."

"Exactly." I removed his hands. "We can do it again and again and again."

"I want to make this last," he said as he sat up. "I've dreamed of nothing but you . . . but this, for so long. I want to memorize every part of you. Every movement. Every breath. Give me that. I want you to forget who you are, bring you to the brink of heaven and hell, until you beg for release."

"I'm begging," I said as I wrapped myself around him.

"But I'm just getting started."

I laughed into the crook of his neck as he picked me up and carried me to the bed.

As I lay there on his fine bed, flushed, my breath heavy in my chest, his gaze melted over my skin. I opened up to him, and he kissed his way up my entire body until he finally threaded his fingers in my hair. He moved slowly, using every part of his body. He was so attuned to me, as if he knew exactly what I wanted, when I wanted it.

Breathing in time, his eyes locked on mine, I didn't care how I looked, what sounds came out of my mouth. We were striving toward a common need—but it was more than need. Everything in our past, present and future was building toward this moment, until a blistering warmth consumed us.

He collapsed beside me and we lay there perfectly still. Empty in a state of bliss. All of the past hurts, all of the pain evaporating into the ether.

All that remained were our bodies—vessels for each other's hearts.

35

"THE PLANS," THE familiar voice whispered in my ear.

I awoke in the middle of the night to find myself alone, although Rhys's scent hung heavy in the air.

Maybe I was dreaming about him or maybe his scent was still on my skin from Spencer's house, but I couldn't escape him.

I slipped out of bed and went to the bathroom. A shower would do me good. I stepped in, feeling the hot water caress my aching muscles. As I washed up, I was so content that I started humming that stupid Backstreet Boys song.

Dane stepped into the bathroom.

"Miss me already?" I asked as I peeked at him over my shoulder.

"Always," he whispered, stepping in behind me, wrapping his arms around my waist, pressing his body against mine.

"What's that tune you were humming?"

"Very funny," I teased. "What, you want me to sing it for you?"

"Of course."

I held up the bar of soap like a microphone. "'You are my fire / the one desire / believe when I say / I want it that way.'"

"That's nice. You'll have to teach it to me."

I turned around, studying him. But he wasn't kidding.

And then I remembered Dane telling me that he held back certain things from Coronado for safekeeping. Did he hold that song back for a reason? So I would know. So I would be able to tell the difference?

Holding his face in my hands, I whispered his name, "Dane." But he just smiled back at me, nothing to suggest he'd slipped away for even a moment. But when I reached out for him, to get a sense of his emotions, I only felt my own reverberating back to me.

That's when I knew. This wasn't Dane. He looked like Dane, acted like Dane, talked like Dane.

But Dane would know that song.

My skin erupted in goose bumps.

"Let me warm you," he said as he arranged my hair around my shoulders.

I thought of him doing that with my hair when Dane let Coronado take over completely after the council dinner . . . and countless other times . . . at the library in New York . . . when we first arrived at the estate. Was Coronado the one who was with me all that time? Last night?

I felt like I was going to be sick. As I looked into his eyes, I wondered whether Dane was even in there at all. Could he see me? Feel me? Or maybe he knew . . . maybe they had an arrangement, some kind of fucked-up love triangle.

"I need to check on Beth," I managed to say as I freed myself from his arms.

He grabbed my hand. "A kiss before you go?"

It took everything I had to do it, but I needed to keep my cool for just a few more minutes. Pressing my lips together, I kissed him, but he forced them open with his tongue. And again there was a part of me, the darkest part of me, that wanted to ignore my instincts. But if I gave in to him, gave in to the darkness, I knew it would be my ruin.

36

AS I LEFT the room, I grabbed a sheet off the bed and wrapped it around me.

Running down the corridor, across the breezeway, down another corridor and up the winding stone steps, I barged into Beth's room to find it empty. On the floor, next to her bed, was a set of blueprints. The same plans Dane had shown her for the wing he was going to build for Rhys. *MP* was printed on the bottom, Max Pinter's logo, along with the date. June 28 of last year. These were drawn up a week after the solstice. How could he have possibly known I would come here? That Rhys would come here? But that wasn't the most troubling thing. The file number printed on the top right-hand corner was the same number I scrawled in red wax at the dinner party. The realization worked its way down my spine until it was undeniable. These were the plans Max Pinter was referring to before he was dragged from the party . . . what Timmons was trying to tell me before he died.

The blueprints indicated that the wing was underground, right below the main floor, not at all where Dane had told Beth it was going to be. I hoped to God I was reaching, trying to make connections that didn't belong together, but I had to know the truth.

Grabbing the plans, I ran down the stairs. As soon as I reached the main hall, the scent of the immortals' blood filled my nostrils. Their stench should've dissipated by now, but it was more than that. Rhys's blood was laced throughout. I'd know that smell anywhere. Was the council still here? Did they somehow get ahold of my brother? Following the scent to the ballroom, I flung the doors open to unleash a sea of blood, the floor littered with bodies. I wanted to run, to close the doors and never come back, but I could smell my brother among them. I had to make sure he wasn't one of the dead. As I waded through the viscera, the bottom of my sheet soaking up their foul blood, I made a point to look at each and every face, frozen in a state of final agony. Mr. and Mrs. Davenport, Mr. and Mrs. Bridges, Mr. Jaeger, all of the immortals and the guards that were left behind to protect them. So many bodies.

I was relieved to find that Rhys wasn't among them, but Lucinda wasn't there, either. I pried a champagne glass from one of the guards' hands and took a whiff. There was no trace of my scent. It was Rhys's blood, and it was fresh, too.

I was racking my brain, trying to figure out how this happened, when I remembered Dane handing the blood bag to the guard, the same guard who went down to fetch the champagne.

What if the guard brought up a different bag? Dane could've swapped those out in a heartbeat. Classic bait and switch—I've seen him do his little magic tricks with rocks, spoons—why not a blood bag? I couldn't help going over every moment I spent with him, trying to decipher who I was really with, but none of that mattered anymore. I'd let myself be distracted by him for the last time.

Dragging the blood-drenched sheet behind me like a corpse, I followed the lines of the blueprints, searching for a possible entry, when I found myself standing in front of a blank wall, the same wall Beth had urinated in front of when we first arrived, the same spot they found her weeping before they locked her away.

I ran my hands over the wall, noticing Lucinda's keys dangling from a false electrical socket.

As I leaned down to turn the key, the wall popped open, sending fresh chills over my entire body.

"Underfoot," I whispered, a hollow sound escaping my throat.

Slipping inside the darkened hallway, down two sets of metal stairs, I came to a glass-paneled door, which led to a small chamber. I peered inside the room; there was a solid metal door on the other side of the room, a half-dozen hazmat suits hanging from hooks in the wall, and a dozen or so metal cylinders lined up against the side wall. As soon as I stepped inside, the door locked behind me, a red light above the metal door on the far end flared, followed by a wet, hissing sound, as a fine mist sprayed down from the vents in the ceiling. It was some kind of hydrogen-peroxide-based solution. It was the same scent I always detected on Lucinda's skin.

I tried to open the metal door on the other side, but it was locked, too.

"Three minutes," a weak voice came from the back corner of the room.

I whipped around to see Lucinda, slumped to the floor, blood seeping from her pores. "That's how long it takes for the disinfection cycle."

"What is this place?" I asked as I tugged at the door.

"All of this was created for you and your brother. A living tomb. We would keep you here, drain you, feed you just enough so you wouldn't wither, but we'd have the disease and the cure. Coronado wanted to rule the council . . . rule the world."

"If my brother's dead," I said as I stalked toward her, "if this is some kind of a trap, I swear to God, I'll kill you."

"I'm already dead," she said as she closed her eyes. "Besides, I have nothing left to lose."

Pulling my hair back from my face, I took in a deep breath through my nose, trying to keep calm. More than anything, I wanted to paint the walls with her blood, but I needed answers. "Why haven't you bled out like the others?" I said as I nudged her foot.

Her eyes fluttered open. "Coronado shared his blood with me—your blood. He said it would protect me. I believed him, because when I gave Rhys's blood to Beth on that first night—"

247

"Wait. That was the medicine you gave her?" I said as I clenched my fists.

"That was before I knew." She attempted to swallow.

"Knew? Knew what? That you're a psycho bitch?" I said as I paced in front of her.

"That Beth wasn't a seer hell-bent on destroying us . . . that you weren't Katia, coming here for revenge, and that your brother was just a boy, a frail, sweet boy, caught in the fray."

"Don't talk about my brother like you know him—like you care about him," I said, my hands aching to be around her throat.

"When Beth didn't die, that was the proof I needed. But it needs to come directly from the source . . . I understand that now. Coronado's blood only carries traces of yours. It wasn't enough to protect me. It only slowed the process. I'm dying just the same."

"Good riddance," I said as I turned away from her, staring up at the red light above the metal door, desperate for it to change.

"He betrayed us both," Lucinda said. "He must've switched the bag. He was always very good with his hands."

"That's disgusting," I said as I glared back at her. "He's your brother. Your twin—"

"You'll never understand what it was like. All those years alone together in this house. He hid me from the world. And as centuries passed, I lost touch with right and wrong, good and bad; he was the only thing I had. But Katia was always hanging over us. My hatred for her clouded my judgment, made me do terrible things, and now I know it was all a lie."

"Do you realize what you've done?"

"I tried to get you to run . . . but you were blinded by his charm . . . blinded by what he wanted you to see. I had no choice but to take matters into my own hands . . . to make you run. But Coronado was always one step ahead of me."

"And what about Timmons and Rennert and Max Pinter and all the other immortals you killed? You're telling me you had no choice?"

"All that was Coronado's doing. He must've followed me to the alchemist's, killing him after I left. I tried to stop Timmons's death, but I was too late. Coronado's been in control all along. Manipulating us. And when I saw what he was doing to Dane—"

"What about what *you* were doing to Dane? You hurt him. I saw what happened. You broke his wrist—"

"Inflicting pain is the only way to make Coronado retreat. My brother loves to inflict pain on others, but he will do anything to avoid the heat of an iron, the slice of a blade, the blow of a fist. Inflict pain and Coronado will hide from it like a coward to let Dane suffer in his place. I was trying to help you . . . both of you. The love you and Dane share is so pure. I've never seen a love like that. I thought I could reason with my brother, but when he married you, took you to his bed—*our* bed—I knew there was no going back." She coughed, splashing blood on the back of her hand. "After sharing a womb, after everything I've done for him, sacrificed for him, he killed me along with the others, as if I were nothing. He wanted to be rid of me so he could have you all to himself, but you saw through him, didn't you?" The slightest hint of a smile passed over her eyes. "You probably realized it wasn't Dane the moment he touched you."

A stab of remorse came over me when I thought about what happened last night. I wanted to believe I was genuinely fooled, caught up in the moment, but I couldn't shake the feeling that, on some level, I knew and did it anyway. The darkest part of me, reaching out for what I thought I truly deserved.

Grabbing one of the chemical tanks, I raised it over my head to bash her head in, when the light turned green. I dropped the canister. "You don't deserve a swift death. You should suffer."

"For once we agree on something." She looked up at me, the pain in her dark eyes piercing right into my soul. I knew that pain . . . the seething guilt pouring out of her matched my own.

37

I YANKED OPEN the metal door, only to find a sterile white room with two hospital beds surrounded by medical equipment. It was sparkling clean, but the smell of blood, urine, morphine, and fear told me everything I couldn't see. But Rhys wasn't there. Just when I was about to turn back to beat the truth out of Lucinda, I heard something—a sound coming from behind a privacy screen—the susurration of breath.

As I stepped toward it, an IV pole came swinging toward my ribs.

Beth reached out to stop it. "It's okay. It's just Ash."

Rhys collapsed in my arms. His head was shaved and he was emaciated to the point where I didn't want to hug him too hard; I didn't want to break him.

Tears streamed down my face. Here he was. My brother. My twin. The better half of me.

He gave me a faint smile, his lips cracking open with the strain.

I wanted him to yell at me. I wanted him to hate me, but he seemed so grateful just to see me. And here I was, in this tiny room with his captor's scent all over my skin. And the worst part was that I could still *feel* Coronado—his mouth against mine, his hands in my hair. Just thinking about last night made me feel all the more wretched and depraved.

"Look," Beth said, "I can touch Rhys . . . I can kiss him. Your blood is magic."

"I'm happy for both of you," I whispered, desperately trying to keep it together.

There was so much hanging between us. I had no idea where to start. How much he remembered . . . how much he knew.

"There's something I need to tell you about Mom . . . she's—"

"I know," he replied.

"How?"

"I felt it. I felt you, too. Slipping away. Every day you became more and more faint. I thought it was me, disappearing, but it was more than that."

And I knew he was speaking of the darkness, taking over. The darkness inside of me that came alive in Coronado's presence.

"But when you came here, I heard your voice. Your footsteps. Your laughter. I knew you'd come for me."

It pained me to think that he was here, *underfoot*, while I . . . well, I couldn't even go there.

"Can you ever forgive me?" I asked.

"There's nothing to forgive." He looked up at me with love in his eyes. "We're together now. That's all that matters."

"That's not *all* that matters." I felt my blood pressure rise. "Coronado has to pay for what he's done."

"I know he hurt you, and I'm sorry I wasn't there for you—"

"This isn't about me. What he did to *me*. This is about you. I can't even think about what he did to you. It's inhuman . . . unforgivable."

He glanced back at the hospital bed, shivering at the sight of it.

"You don't have to talk about what happened, but if you ever need—"

"When I ran out of the corn that day, I was going to get help. I found Teresa and Spencer. I told them everything that was happening and they said they wanted to help me, help us. He made a phone call . . . said it was someone he knew . . . someone who could help. About twenty minutes later, a black SUV pulled up; we got in. I saw the mark on the driver's wrist—the same mark that Dane had—and that's the last time I remember walking, talking, feeling the wind, feeling the sun," he said as he looked longingly toward the exit.

"We have to get out of here," I said, thinking of Coronado, what he would do if he found us.

"We've been trying, but he can't walk," Beth said.

"Why?" I looked over his legs. They were thin, but there didn't seem to be any breaks.

"He hasn't been out of that bed for a year."

"B-but I saw him on the footage," I sputtered. "In the wheelchair, that was a week ago."

"That was from a *year* ago," Beth said. "When Spencer first delivered Rhys to Coronado."

My chin quivered. "You mean . . . he's been *here* all this time?"

Beth nodded.

I thought of all the times I passed by the entrance, without even a glimmer of recognition. Finding him was everything I'd longed for in the past year, to feel whole again, but the darkness must've clouded my senses.

"I can walk," Rhys said as he tried to stand, but he only folded in on himself like a newborn colt. Beth and I tried to brace him, but he groaned in anguish when we made contact with his back.

I looked to see what was causing him so much pain, and when I saw the bedsores, I had to grit my teeth to stop myself from going into the other room to beat the last bit of life out of Lucinda. How could anyone do this to another human being . . . and to someone as good as Rhys?

"What can we do?" Beth asked.

"My blood," I said as I grabbed a scalpel from one of the trays to cut my wrist, but my brother stopped me.

I could've forced it down his throat, but I didn't want him to have to endure one more thing against his will.

"It will heal you," I explained. "You'll be able to walk out of here on your own two feet."

"I don't want it. No more blood."

"Rhys, you have open wounds. A lot of them," I said as I looked down at the needle marks all over his body, some infected, some well on their way.

"To leave this place, you're going to come in contact with a lot of people. If anyone besides us has contact with your blood, they'll die."

Watching the realization come over him, the reminder of what he was, what his blood could do, was like a dagger in the heart.

"Just close your eyes if you're squeamish."

"No, it's not that. I'm over my fear of blood. That's been my entire life this past year," he said as he glanced over at the endless array of extraction equipment.

"Then what is it?"

"I don't . . . I don't want to be . . ."

"Oh," I whispered, the realization crushing down on me like a heavy weight. He was afraid of becoming like Dane or Lucinda. He was afraid of becoming like *me*. I swallowed back my tears.

"My blood will heal you. Nothing more. You won't become immortal. All it will do is make you feel strong for a little while, seal any open wounds, help with the atrophy and the morphine withdrawal. But it won't prevent you from getting hurt in the future."

Rhys looked to Beth.

She smiled at him, chipped tooth and all. She didn't see his hollow cheeks, his sunken eyes, his decaying flesh. She saw Rhys, the way he was before. And I thought: This is what real love looks like. *This.*

"I won't do it to ease my pain," Rhys said. "But I'll do it so I won't hurt anyone else. I don't think I could bear it."

He leaned back against Beth; I slit my wrist, then placed it up to his mouth. "Just this once," he said.

As my blood flowed into him, I tried to bury my feelings of guilt and rage and remorse—there would be no secrets between us after this, but at least my blood could do something good for a change.

Watching the wounds on Rhys's body heal brought fresh tears to my eyes. And when the soft peach color returned to his face, I knew he was going to be okay. He had a long way to go until he was completely healthy again, but this was a start. Beth helped him to his feet. He was stiff and slow, but able to walk.

We had to pass through the decontamination chamber to leave. As we closed the heavy metal door behind us, the mist began to fall.

"Are we going home?" Rhys asked.

I thought about what that would be like, taking him back to New York City. Without our mother there, and with Timmons gone, it was just an apartment. Nothing more. But we also had to worry about Coronado now. And New York City would be the first place he'd look.

"We have money. Lots of it. Maybe we can buy an island somewhere. Just the three of us—"

"He'll find you, Ashlyn," Lucinda said from the back corner.

Rhys cowered at the sound of her voice.

"Coronado will never let you go. He will use your love for Rhys and Beth to control you. They will never be safe. You must end this now or accept the consequences."

"Shut your mouth." I glared at Lucinda, whose breath had become so shallow, her color so pale, that I knew she was barely clinging to life.

"I know a way . . . a way you can all be together again. A way that I can be with Coronado."

"Don't listen to her," I said as I stared up at the light over the door, willing it to change.

"Ironic that this is where I'll die. No matter how many times that disinfection cycle goes off, I will never be clean. I will never be clean of what I've done to you and Rhys. The sins I've committed in my own brother's name."

I was trying to ignore her, but Rhys whispered, "Can you help her?"

"Help her?" I balked. "Isn't this the woman who helped torture you for the past year, drained your blood, starved you, drugged you?"

Rhys swallowed hard. "That's true. But she's also the one who brought Beth down here to find me. She wants to do the right thing."

"She deserves to die."

As the light changed from red to green, and the mist stopped, I opened the door.

"Please, Ash." Rhys placed his emaciated hand on my shoulder and looked back at Lucinda. "I don't want my blood to be the cause of any more deaths."

I would've been happy to let her drown in a pool of her own fetid blood, but I couldn't turn my back on my brother's wishes. If this would help ease his conscience, I'd do it.

I walked over to Lucinda, kicking the canister out of my way.

"You have my brother to thank for your pathetic life," I said, revealing the scalpel secreted in the palm of my hand.

"I know how to make amends." The words rattled from the depths of her throat. "The alchemist . . . he told me a way."

I couldn't stand listening to one more lie come out of her mouth. Using the scalpel, I slit open her palm, and then my own, grasping her hand in violent mercy.

I wanted to hate her . . . I wanted to despise her, but as my blood penetrated her heart, a powerful wave of memories and emotions washed over me.

Holding a young boy in the dark, protecting him from a man stalking the halls with a whip in his hands.

Lying in bed, burning up with fever, as a beautiful young man tended to her, feeding her tiny sips of immortal blood from the same amulet she carried now. The young man was Coronado, before he met Katia, before this darkness befell their house. "I'm going to find the immortal whose blood this belongs to," he whispered. "And then we can be together forever."

For years she waited, growing frailer by the day, and when he finally returned to the crumbling castle, he hadn't aged a day, but he had certainly changed. A cruelty she hardly recognized. Dragging the alchemist behind him, he'd forced him to make Lucinda immortal.

Promises were made . . . and broken. Whispers in the dark were contorted into the ultimate taboo. Isolation led to madness.

And when Katia's portrait was hung in the study, I felt her rage every time she gazed upon it.

But when Beth and I arrived at the castle, doubt began to

slip under her skin. Along with a guilt so crushing, I thought it might bury me alive.

In the early morning hours, she stole away to visit Rennert at the apothecary. I heard his words of warning. "You're twins, the perfect vessel. There isn't a better match to be made in heaven or hell. There will be deep sacrifice. You must accept the light in order to step into darkness. But in that darkness, you will be whole again. You will be new. You will find redemption and peace inside the pain."

Lucinda was telling the truth about everything. I could feel it. See it. She was just as much a victim of Coronado as the rest of us. Maybe more. To be betrayed by your family . . . your twin . . . I couldn't even fathom that kind of despair.

As we started to heal, I wanted to keep cutting deeper and deeper, to see every last detail, but when I looked into Lucinda's eyes, I knew she'd seen my memories as well. I knew she'd had enough.

"I saw what your mother did for you," Lucinda said. "The light she left inside you. You can use it to take Coronado from Dane's body and place him inside of *me*. I can be his vessel."

"And then what?" I asked. "He'll take you the same way he's taken Dane. I know firsthand what it's like to be the vessel for another soul, and there's only darkness."

"We can control him with pain." She squeezed my hands. "Coronado will run from it, but I can take it long enough—"

"Long enough for what? You're immortal, and you now carry my blood. I won't be able to stop you."

"It's true. I cannot die. But there are worse things than death for an immortal."

The house seemed to groan in accord.

Our eyes locked, and in that moment, I knew exactly what she meant. *Immurement.*

I always thought Katia was the one who left something inside of me, but it was really my mother. Her light. And now I realized that I could use that light to take Coronado from Dane's body and bind him to Lucinda, but if I gave away my light, it would mean darkness for me, and Lucinda knew it, too. But when I looked back at my brother and Beth, when I thought of Dane being at the mercy of Coronado's cruel whims, I knew what I had to do.

"If we go through with this, I have one demand," I said to Lucinda.

"Anything."

"When I use the light inside of me to do this, and the darkness takes over, I need you to take me with you. The three of us will be immured together. I've seen what the darkness can do to a person. I won't replace one monster for another."

She looked at me in quiet anguish. "You have my word."

My eyes welled up with tears. It was confirmation of everything I'd feared. She'd seen into my soul. What I would become. And it scared her.

38

AS BETH TOOK Rhys outside, Lucinda and I loaded up as many canisters as we could carry, placing them strategically around the main floor.

Grabbing a butcher's knife, a box of matches, and a large tin of kerosene from the kitchen, Lucinda left a trail of accelerant behind her. "This should draw Dane to the surface. Burns take the longest to heal."

"Are you sure you want to go through with this?" I asked her. "Maybe there's another way, in time—"

"Coronado and I should've died long ago," Lucinda replied. "This is where we belong. Together. Forever."

"Blood and salt," I whispered. Theirs was an intense love, a destructive kind of love that I didn't want anymore. We'd all done enough damage to one another.

"I'll let you do the honors," she said, handing me the box of matches.

Taking one last look, at the grandeur, the history around me, I opened the doors to Coronado's study and regarded Katia's portrait. The original sin. The way she was looking over her shoulder, waiting with bated breath for the touch of a man who would be her ruin.

And in that moment, I knew what had driven her to make an alliance with the Dark Spirit in the first place. I understood it better than anyone.

Doing this might destroy me, but I'd have to take that chance. For Rhys and Beth and Dane . . . but also for Katia, my mother, and every Larkin girl who'd fallen before me.

I'd rather go dark in a blaze of glory than waste a hundred years stoking a dying ember.

I struck a flame, the smell of phosphorous and fear nipping at the edge of my senses. Instead of tossing the match haphazardly, I moved in close, setting flame to the far corner of the painting, watching it spread and grow, not unlike the poison Coronado sowed through my bloodline.

In a daze, I watched the fire catch the trail of kerosene, tracking it all the way up the grand staircase to his quarters.

"Fool me once, shame on me.

"Fool me twice . . .

"I burn your shit to the ground."

As I crossed the threshold, the flames licked my skin, my hair, but I welcomed the pain.

Pain was the only thing that would keep Dane with me.

39

IT WAS JUST before dawn when I stepped outside. Night was still desperately trying to hang on to the horizon, but the sun was unstoppable.

And that's exactly how *I* felt.

Caught between the light and the dark.

When I looked at Beth and Rhys huddled together on the seashell path, it brought tears to my eyes. If I slipped into darkness, not only would I be trapped with Lucinda and Coronado in immurement, in eternal agony, but I'd miss out on so much. The children Beth and Rhys might have, their grandchildren, the generations to come. I wondered if I was making a huge mistake, but I knew this was my last chance at redemption.

As much as it hurt to admit, Dane, Beth, and Rhys could live without me, but they wouldn't live long if Coronado had his way.

Maybe there was a part of me that could live vicariously

through them. Through our blood. During my immurement, if I concentrated hard enough, I might be able to feel the sun on my face, taste sea salt on the tip of my tongue. Smell wildflowers and freshly tilled soil. It may not seem like much, but in the darkness, a glimmer is all you need to hold on to life . . . to love.

My brother slipped his bony hand into mine, startling me. "Whatever you're about to do, you don't have to do this . . . We can run . . . we can—"

"Mom gave me this light when she saved me. All this time I thought it was for me . . . to keep the darkness at bay, but it was really for this moment, for you and Beth . . . and Dane."

"But—"

"I need you to trust me. I know I've said that before and—"

"Always." He squeezed my hand.

It almost broke my heart how willing he was to put everything on the line for me. After everything we've been through, everything I've done. "You were always the good part of me, and as long as you walk this earth, a part of me can live in the light. Just knowing you and Beth and Dane will be safe and happy and free. That's enough. If the darkness consumes me and I'm immured along with them, I may not be able to see you . . . or touch you, but I'll be there. In your blood. In your heart."

I looked at Lucinda, kneeling in front of an olive tree, and I wondered what she was praying for—Mercy? Justice? Forgiveness?—but when I reached out to her, I found she was praying for strength.

We were all making a great sacrifice for this to come to pass.

And if the darkness consumed me, Lucinda would have to take me with her. Here, we would remain in this living tomb, where the only people we could hurt were each other.

Using the scalpel, I slit open the palms of my hands, coaxing my blood forward. As soon as it made contact with the soil, I felt connected to the vortex churning beneath my feet. Beth was right. This was a place of great and terrible energy, just like Quivira. Darkness thrived here.

As I walked a wide circle, preparing for the ritual, I couldn't help thinking of my mother. I hoped she would be proud of me. I hoped she and Timmons were together now, watching over us.

The moment I stepped inside the completed circle, it felt as if my ribs were being spread apart for extra air. It hurt, but the relief was overwhelming.

The spirit world was answering my call. I felt life and death trembling from my fingertips.

As much as I craved revenge, this was about Rhys and Beth and Dane—keeping them safe from that monster, and the monster I may become.

And all I had to do was let go of the light and let the darkness in.

But everything inside me wanted to hold on. That light was the last connection I had to my mother—without it, what would I be?

It was time to find out.

40

I DIDN'T NEED to look back to know that Dane had emerged from the castle. The scent of burning flesh and hair flared in my nostrils, but it went deeper than that. I felt his pain . . . his confusion . . . his remorse pulsing through me.

But as he approached, I felt something unexpected. Dane. Not the slivers of Dane that Coronado had been meting out, but all of him, all at once—a crippling wave of despair and heartache.

And there was part of me—a very sick part—that wanted to believe Coronado was gone for good, that we didn't have to go through with this, but that's exactly what Coronado wanted, what the Dark Spirit wanted. Dane was nothing but a sacrificial lamb.

"Ashlyn." He stumbled into the circle, his flesh shriveled from his bones, his hair singed beyond recognition. "Whatever happened . . . whatever he did, we can work through this."

"You don't know," I said with a sharp inhalation of breath. "You don't know what he's done?"

"I must've lost control. The last thing I remember is asking you to marry me. And you said yes," he recalled with a hazy smile of remembrance. "And then there was darkness. When I came back, I was on fire."

It was sickening to watch him in so much pain, but he had to know the truth.

"You married me. You killed Spencer before he could tell me the truth about Coronado . . . and then we . . . I . . . I slept with you . . . but it wasn't *you*. And then I discovered all the immortals—you killed them with Rhys's blood. You've been keeping my brother in a torture chamber . . . underfoot." I winced. "All that time he was right below my feet. And you were going to imprison me next to him, so you could control the cure and the curse."

"No," he murmured as he staggered back, his flesh slowly starting to regenerate. "That wasn't me. I can promise you with everything that I am . . . everything that I have, I didn't know. He fooled me just as much as he fooled you. But this is me," he said, tears streaming down his cheeks. "Tell me you feel it . . . tell me you know the difference."

"For now, but as soon as your flesh heals, Coronado will take over again."

"I don't understand."

"The only way to force Coronado to give up control is pain. That's why Lucinda was hurting you. She was trying to help us."

As he looked down at his body beginning to heal, he said, "I can stay in control. I can do this."

"You have no idea how much I want that to be true, but when it comes to you and Coronado, everything we feel . . . everything inside of us is a betrayal."

Looking at his ravaged face, his twisted body, pained me. This wasn't the boy I'd fallen in love with. This was what loving me did to him. Did to us all.

"But I can fix this. I can help you," I said. "I'm going to use my light to take Coronado from you and put him in Lucinda. She wants this. He's her twin."

Dane looked confused at first, but when he realized what this meant for me, what giving away my light would do to me, he panicked. "If you use your mother's light, the darkness could consume you."

"I have to take that chance. If I go dark, Lucinda has agreed to take me with her, but you'll need to let me go."

"I can't."

"You can and you will. This is bigger than you and me. Promise me you'll look after them." I glanced back at Rhys and Beth, holding hands just outside the circle.

"Of course," Dane replied. "But you need to promise me something in return," he said as his hair began to grow back, the burns healing on his face. "There's light inside of you that's yours alone. I saw it in Quivira, long before your mother saved you. Find it. Hang on to it. Not for me . . . not for Beth and Rhys, but for yourself. Because you're worthy of it. Believe in that."

Dane clutched his stomach, dropping to his knees, and when he looked up at me, I felt the tiniest shift.

"I come to you in amends," he said.

"Amends?" I studied him, trying to discern every detail. "Dane would never say something like that."

"It's me. What do I have to do to prove that?" he said, looking at me with nothing but love in his eyes.

"That's the thing." I shook my head rapidly as I backed away, tears blurring my vision. "There's nothing you can do or say. Neither one of us can be trusted anymore."

As I raised my hands toward the sky, he got to his feet. "What are you doing?"

"I've been holding on to my mother's light all this time, for this reason. I'm going to rip you from Dane's body. It's time to end this" he said.

"Go ahead, waste your light—the darkness suits you—but without a vessel, it's a pointless exercise. I can think of so many better ways to exert your energy. Really, *mi amor*, all of my relations are dead. I saw to that. Do you take me for a fool?"

"I do, actually," Lucinda said as she emerged from the olive grove, stepping inside the circle. "Did you forget about me? Your dear sister . . . your twin?"

All the blood seemed to leach from his face, but he tried to cover his shock the best he could. "Thank God you're all right, Lucinda. I was horrified to learn what Dane tried to do to you, but I knew you were too smart to fall for that parlor trick."

"But I did. Oh, how I fell," she said. "But Ash saved me, and there's no better vessel in the world than a twin. Just think, we'll be together, as we once were inside the womb."

"That's madness," he said. He tried to force a laugh, but the tremor in his voice gave him away. "Let's be civilized about this. We can work out a schedule. A time-share, if you will. Two nights with Dane, two nights with me. You two can fight over who gets me for the extra night."

"That's very generous," I said. "But I think we're good with this. Right, Lucinda?"

"I've been waiting nearly five hundred years for this moment."

Coronado attempted a smile. "I had no idea the two of you had grown so close in that special way, but I suppose I can work with that. It's good to have a change every once in a while. The three of us can go to France—I think they're much more accepting of that lifestyle."

"I have somewhere else in mind," Lucinda said. "A little closer to home."

"*Ego sum qui pecavvi*," I whispered in his ear. "I am he who has sinned."

"No . . . no," Coronado murmured right before he turned and tried to run, but the circle wouldn't release him. "Anything but that. Anything but immurement. I'll do anything you ask. I'll—"

Jabbing the scalpel into his stomach, I twisted it until Dane came back to me.

"Immure *me*," he panted. "As I am, with Coronado inside of

270

me. There's no reason to give away your light. Let me do this for you . . . while I can still make that choice."

"Haven't we suffered enough?" I kissed his trembling lips for the last time. "It's time for you to be free."

"But without you . . . ," he gasped.

"Fight to stay in your body, and I promise you, I'll fight the darkness inside of me."

He nodded, tears streaming down his face. "Ashlyn," he whispered one last time.

"Dane," I whispered back.

As I pulled out the scalpel, Dane slumped over in pain, clutching his stomach, and I took my place in the center of the circle.

Breathing in the magic all around me, I spoke Katia's words.

As I chanted the spell, I watched in amazement as a golden glow began to beam from my skin . . . just as vibrant as my mother's light when she took Katia's soul from me. At first, it pulsed forward in fits and spurts, but then it became a steady flow, reaching straight into Dane's chest. Lifting him in the air, I felt his heart as if it were beating in the palm of my hand.

Fight him, Dane. Don't give in.

Opening myself up, I thought of every good memory I had of Dane—when we first met at the junkyard and he brushed his thumb against my hip bone . . . how I used only my senses to find him at the wreathing ceremony . . . sitting with him by the fire . . . holding his hand in the corn . . . the way he carried me into the lake, washing the blood from my skin . . . our first real kiss . . . being with him under Heartbreak Tree—and the light grew stronger, enfolding him, protecting him. Using the last of my mother's light, I coaxed the darkness toward me, lulling it out of Dane's body, until a slow black ooze of smoke began to seep from Dane's mouth. Coronado's soul. Without hesitation, Lucinda stepped toward Dane, inhaling deeply, taking Coronado's sickness into her lungs, as if she were born to it. She kissed Dane with such ferocious need that it made me woozy. Love and hate. Hurt and betrayal. Possession and rage, swirling all around them.

Dane's body convulsed and buckled beneath her lips, but Lucinda held on tight, until there was nothing left. And when Lucinda finally let go, both Dane and me collapsed to the ground like empty shells, staring across the circle at each other.

As the light began to fade from my skin, I closed my eyes. I couldn't bear to look at him as I turned into a monster. As I lay there feeling the darkness slip between my bones, infecting every cell in my body, I caught a sliver of light. At first I wasn't sure if it was a mirage or an errant ray of sunlight seeping through my eyelids, but the more I homed in on that light, the stronger it beamed. And inside that tiny sliver were memories—Rhys and Beth, all dressed up, exchanging rings under a canopy of honeysuckle; little kids running around, with Beth's eyes, my brother's smile; Dane and me holding hands on the edge of a cliff, staring off into a never-ending horizon—and I realized none of these things had happened. They were images of the future—one that didn't include me being immured with Lucinda and Coronado.

The darkness was still there, it always would be, but if I concentrated on that sliver of light inside of me, I could nurture it, make it grow, fill it with new memories. There would still be death and heartache and sorrow—that's just a part of life, but I could choose to live in the light every single day.

As I crawled over to Dane, I asked, "Is it you?" But I didn't need to. I could feel him all at once, the sorrow, the tenderness, the love crushing down on him. On me.

"Yes," he said, weeping, still unable to fully move. "And it's you," he said, straining to touch me with his fingertips.

All that remained were the best parts of us, reaching out to each other in forgiveness, hope, and love.

I was nearly there when I was jerked back.

Whipping my head around, I saw Lucinda, dragging me by my ankle out of the circle.

"Lucinda, stop! It's Ash. I can stay. I won't hurt them. There's still light inside of me."

"You belong to me," she said, but the cold veneer in her eyes gave it away. This wasn't Lucinda anymore. It was Coronado.

Twisting my body around, I jabbed the scalpel into her leg.

"I don't belong to anyone," I said, digging it all the way in until I hit bone.

After a few tortured seconds, I watched a softness pass over her face as Lucinda returned to me.

"This is where we part ways," she said as she stared off into the horizon, as if she were trying to memorize every last detail. With her black hair, wild and loose, the sun rising in her eyes, I'd never seen her more at peace, more beautiful.

"I'm sorry," I said, my eyes welling up with tears at the sacrifice she was making.

"This isn't the end. It's a new beginning . . . for all of us. How it was meant to be."

As she turned to limp toward the burning castle, her blood seeping down her leg, into the soil, I swore I could hear worms and maggots rise to the surface, in the wake of her footsteps, feeding on one another in an endless cycle of life and death.

With each step closer, the wind grew stronger, the ground trembled, and by the time she reached the entry, the energy encircling the castle had reached a fever pitch.

But I wasn't the one doing this. Maybe it was the Dark Spirit, welcoming them home.

And the moment Lucinda stepped over the threshold, disappearing into the veil of flames, a huge explosion ripped through the wreckage. The ground grumbled in defiance until it finally gave way, opening up like the deadliest bloom, swallowing the castle whole, then sealing back up again.

And then there was silence.

Not a crow to be heard.

As we stood there, staring out over the barren patch of land, tiny flecks of white began to fall all around us. It looked like snow, but it wasn't cold. I caught one of the flakes on my finger-tip, to find it was only ash.

A surge of raw emotion rushed through me, through all of us.

"Is this what you saw in your vision?" I asked Beth. "The four of us together under a snowy sky that wasn't cold?"

"Isn't it beautiful?" She smiled as she twirled around.

"It is." I let out an unexpected laugh.

Dane reached out, removing a speck of ash from my eyelashes.

The gesture was so simple, so sweet, it nearly brought me to my knees.

I looked up at him, expecting to feel that familiar push and pull, but it was gone now. It wasn't about our blood anymore—light and dark, me bending to him or him bending to me—it was about being together as equals, standing side by side in our pain. It wasn't perfect. But it was real.

It felt good knowing that from here on out, nothing was predestined or left to fate. Our future belonged to no one but ourselves. Whatever we made of it.

The black silk ribbon curled through the air, but it passed right by us to dance over the barren spot of land, the place of Coronado and Lucinda's immurement. That kind of love didn't belong to us anymore. Without it, I felt untethered. I felt free.

I couldn't help thinking of the first time my brother and I stood in front of the corn at Quivira.

"Remember when I told you that it was good to be afraid? That it meant you still had something to live for?"

Rhys slipped his hand into mine, squeezing tight.

"I'm not afraid anymore. Of anything." Tears streamed down my cheeks, but I didn't wipe them away. "I don't need the fear anymore to know I'm alive," I said as I looked at every single one of them. "I have love instead."

Saying good-bye to the blood and salt of my youth, my heart of ash, I turned my back on the past and set out to become the woman I wanted to be.

ACKNOWLEDGMENTS

TO MY EDITOR, Arianne Lewin, thank you for believing in me . . . in Ash and Dane. You taught me a tremendous amount about writing, revising and the business of publishing. I'm forever grateful.

Thanks to my copy editor, Anne Heausler, my cover designers, Theresa Evangelista and Jessica Jenkins, and everyone at Putnam for getting this book to the shelves.

To my godsend of an agent, Jaida Temperly, thank you for everything you do. Every single day. And to everyone at New Leaf, I'm incredibly lucky to have you in my corner.

Special thanks to Josh Adams for making all this possible.

I cherish the time I spent at the Coronado Quivira Museum in Lyons, Kansas, and Castell d'Emporda in Spain—thanks for letting me have run of the place.

To my friends Alexis Bass, Rebecca Behrens, Virginia

Boecker, Libba Bray, Gina Carey, Sona Charaiporta, Dhonielle Clayton, Bess Cozby, Melissa Gray, Maggie Hall, Lee Kelly, Jodi Kendall, Erin Morgenstern, Danielle Paige, Veronica Rossi, Kate Scelsa, Adam Scott, Eric Smith, Courtney Stevens, Nova Ren Suma, Kara Thomas, Jen Marie Thorne, April Tucholke, Jasmine Warga—for the record, I would help every single one of you bury a body. Call me.

And to my family, Maddie, Rahm, John, Joyce, Cristie, and last but not least, Honeypie.